P.

A

After the rescue team had nearly given up hope of anyone being found alive, the first live victim has been discovered in the Baghdad Sheraton Hotel, destroyed by suicide bombers. Delaney Carson, famed photojournalist, was discovered early yesterday morning. Carson and her partner, the now deceased Pulitzer Prize-winning Reid Davis, were in Iraq to report on the war efforts for Interstar News.

The blast rocked the stately structure near midnight Tuesday, reducing the hotel to rubble. Carson's survival adjusts the assumed death toll to seventy-one.

The majority of the hotel's occupants were foreign journalists. There has been speculation that the Sheraton was targeted because insurgents believed it to be used as a secret command post for the American military, a rumor the Pentagon denies.

Carson was stabilized and flown to Kuwait for medical assistance. Her condition could not be verified.

Dear Reader,

The leaves aren't the only things changing colors this October. Starting this month, you'll notice Silhouette Intimate Moments is evolving into its vibrant new look, and that's just the start of some exciting changes we're undergoing. As of February 2007, we will have a new name, Silhouette Romantic Suspense. Not to worry, these are still the breathtaking romances—don't forget the suspense!—that you've come to know and love in Intimate Moments. Keep your eyes open for our new look over the next few months as we transition fully to our new appearance. As always, we deliver on our promise of romance, danger and excitement.

Speaking of romance, danger and excitement, award-winning author Ruth Wind brings us *Juliet's Law* (#1435), the debut of her miniseries SISTERS OF THE MOUNTAIN. An attorney must depend on a handsome tribal officer to prove her sister's innocence on murder charges. Wendy Rosnau continues her arresting SPY GAMES series with *Undercover Nightingale* (#1436) in which an explosives expert falls for an undercover agent and learns just how deceiving looks can be.

You'll nearly swoon as a Navajo investigator protects a traumatized photojournalist in *The Last Warrior* (#1437) by Kylie Brant. Don't miss Loreth Anne White's new miniseries, SHADOW SOLDIERS, and its first story, *The Heart of a Mercenary* (#1438), a gripping tale with a to-die-for alpha hero!

This month, and every month, let our stories sweep you into an exciting world of passion and suspense. Happy reading!

Sincerely,

Patience Smith
Associate Senior Editor

Please address questions and book requests to:
Silhouette Reader Service
U.S.: 3010 Walden Ave., P.O. Box 1325, Buffalo, NY 14269
Canadian: P.O. Box 609, Fort Erie, Ont. L2A 5X3

Kylie Brant

THE LAST WARRIOR

Silhouette®

INTIMATE MOMENTS™

Published by Silhouette Books
America's Publisher of Contemporary Romance

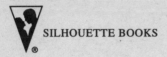 **SILHOUETTE BOOKS**

ISBN-13: 978-0-373-27507-6
ISBN-10:   0-373-27507-2

THE LAST WARRIOR

Copyright © 2006 by Kimberly Bahnsen

Visit Silhouette Books at www.eHarlequin.com

Printed in U.S.A.

Books by Kylie Brant

Silhouette Intimate Moments

†*Hard To Handle* #1108
Born in Secret #1112
†*Hard To Resist* #1119
†*Hard To Tame* #1125
***Alias Smith and Jones* #1169
**Entrapment #1221
**Truth or Lies #1238
***Dangerous Deception* #1306
In Sight of the Enemy #1323
Close to the Edge #1341
The Business of Strangers #1366
The Last Warrior #1437

†Charmed and Dangerous
**The Tremaine Tradition

KYLIE BRANT

Kylie Brant is the award-winning author of twenty-two novels. When she's not dreaming up stories of romance and suspense, she works as an elementary teacher for learning disabled students. Kylie has dealt with her newly empty nest by filling the house with even more books, and won't be satisfied until those five vacant bedrooms are full of them!

Kylie invites readers to check out her Web site at www.kyliebrant.com. You can contact her by writing to P.O. Box 231, Charles City, IA 50616, or e-mailing her at kyliebrant@hotmail.com.

For my first grandbaby, Rylan Jace, who already
holds my heart in his sweet little hands.

Acknowledgements:

Special thanks go to Norman Koren, photographer
extraordinaire, who is always endlessly patient with
the photography-challenged; and to Larry DiLucchio,
for his wonderfully factual Web site, and his generosity
of time in answering questions about Navajo culture.
Any errors in the story are undoubtedly due to my
not asking the right questions!

Chapter 1

"You need to get laid."

Joe Youngblood shot a narrowed look at Arnie Benally as they crossed the Navajo Tribal Police parking lot toward their cars. Correctly interpreting the danger in his colleague's glare, Arnie held up his hand placatingly. "Okay, hear me out. All I'm saying is this whole disagreement with your grandfather isn't like you. Most of us don't like the Tribal Council's decision to bring in a *belagana* to write this book on Navajo culture, but is it really worth being at odds with Charley over? You have different opinions. End of story."

"And this involves a woman…how?"

"You're too tightly wound, man." They paused beside Joe's unmarked blue Jeep, and Arnie winked.

"What you need is a night of hot, mind-numbing sex with some sweet young thing to clear your head. Sex relieves stress. There's research."

"That's charming," Joe said drily. He dug in the pocket of his jeans for the keys. "Now I can see how you convinced Brenda to marry you. You've got the heart of a poet."

"Brenda would agree with me." But Arnie cast a quick glance over his shoulder, as if half expecting to see his short plump wife behind him. "She's even mentioned fixing you up sometime. She's got a friend who's…" Meeting Joe's gaze again, his words trailed off.

But the only sign of Joe's temper was the tightness with which he clenched the keys in his fist. His voice when he spoke was mild. "I'm capable of finding my own woman. And I'll take your other suggestion… under advisement."

"Sure." Arnie shrugged, and started edging toward his own vehicle. "I—we—just want the best for you, Joe. You know."

"Yeah. I know." Opening the driver's door of his Jeep, Joe slid inside. He slammed the door with a bit more force than necessary, but he wasn't really angry with Arnie. They'd known each other too long to stay annoyed every time the other man's mouth ran ahead of his brain.

But the thought of anyone, even his friends, discussing his private life made Joe wince. His separation last year had started the public speculation; the final divorce decree four months ago had fueled it. The Navajo

Nation lands encompassed an area the size of West Virginia. But its grapevine was as reliable as Mayberry's.

He started the car and drove off the lot. He wondered if it was the gossip that had driven Heather, his ex, to move out of Tuba City a few weeks ago. But such conjecture was useless. If he hadn't been able to figure out what she was thinking in the last few months of their marriage, he sure wasn't going to be any more successful now. He was long past the point of caring, at any rate.

The only thing he did care about was that she'd taken his son with her.

The familiar burn settled in his chest, spreading. Having joint custody abruptly reduced to every other weekend wasn't something he planned on accepting. But until the new hearing date arrived, Heather had effectively limited his options.

He smiled grimly, remembering Arnie's earlier words. The man had been correct about one thing. It was time to make peace with his grandfather. Their relationship had always been too close to let a minor disagreement come between them.

But as for the rest of Arnie's advice…Joe shook his head. It was a female who'd caused all his problems. The last thing he needed was another woman in his life. For any reason.

It was nearly dusk when Joe pulled up to his grandfather's log hogan just outside Tuba City. Noticing the single light on inside, he abruptly remembered that tonight was Monday, Charley Youngblood's poker night. If Joe's grandfather followed his usual routine, he wouldn't be back until nearly midnight, after doing his best to fleece those he called his closest friends. Joe may as well head for home. Fence-mending was going to have to wait until tomorrow.

But as he drove away, Joe found the thought of home particularly unappealing. The house always seemed emptier following one of his weekends with Jonny. It seemed filled with the hollow echoes of his son's voice. His constant questions. His high-pitched squeals and shouts of triumph when he beat Joe, as he was all too apt to do, in a video game. The clever arguments he came up with to avoid bedtime, which showed a devious ingenuity beyond his five years.

Those echoes could ambush a man when exhaustion had lowered his defenses. Could play on his deepest fears and fan them into full-blown panic. Joe wasn't going to be a weekend father permanently. Some days, clinging to that belief was the only thing that kept him sane.

But it was the threat of those echoes that now had him avoiding home. Rather than taking the turn that would eventually carry him to his house, he veered west, deliberately blanking his mind.

He and Arnie, part of a multiagency task force, were close to an arrest in the crystal meth case they were working and they'd worked later than usual. Dusk was already settling over the area, constructing shadows out of the cottonwoods and juniper trees that posted sentry in the vast space between houses. Housing developments were becoming more common on Navajo lands, but many of the people, including himself, valued a more isolated existence.

He drove nearly ten minutes without passing another vehicle. Lights winked in the distance, and he frowned, slowing. Charley Youngblood owned a handful of rental properties in and around Tuba City. The place ahead belonged to Charley, but Joe knew that it should have been empty. He'd personally escorted the former tenants off the property himself after they'd failed for months to pay rent.

His grandfather had a weakness for sob stories and false promises, but after twelve years on the job, Joe was far more cynical. Either the former tenants had sneaked back in or someone else had decided to take advantage of a vacant building in a remote area.

Joe eased off the road several hundred yards from the house, and cut the lights. Switching off the ignition, he got out and jogged up to the property. There wasn't a vehicle out front, so he continued around the house. He didn't find one in back, either.

Silently climbing the porch steps, he peered in the window. He had a partial view into the kitchen, which appeared empty.

Retracing his steps, he circled around the front and knocked on the door. When no one answered, he pounded again, this time with restrained force.

Still no answer.

Joe smiled grimly. If the unlawful occupant inside meant to ignore him, he or she had a very big surprise in store for them. He reached up for the porch roof overhang. Finding the extra key always kept there, within moments he had the door swinging open.

Delaney Carson was lost in a world of her own making, seventies rock screaming through the headphones of her iPod, a computer screen full of images, and her mind flooded with half-formed ideas. Each new project was like this, an exciting, gut-clenching anticipation of possibilities. But this one represented her return to the land of the living, after existing for far too long in a self-induced numbed haze.

After two years, it was about damn time.

She'd been afraid accepting the job would be a mistake. That she wasn't ready. Or capable. A myriad of fears had festered in the last twenty-four months, sly fingers of torment that clawed through every ounce of confidence. She hadn't conquered all the fears, but she'd conquered the addiction that fed them, and she wanted—needed—to step forward. This had been the step she'd chosen.

The memory card on her digital camera had been full by the time she arrived, and it was those images she sorted through now, already considering a possible organizational format for the book.

Sting was pleading with Roxanne as Delaney peered more closely at the screen. Since her hips were firmly planted in the chair, she moved her shoulders in rhythm to the music as she selected and docked photos. Pursing her lips, she was considering whether to trash a photo with poor light quality when she found herself in the dark. Literally.

Force of habit had her pressing the save command on the computer, heaving a sigh of relief when it did so successfully. Obviously the electricity wasn't off. Maybe the overhead bulb needed to be replaced. She pushed her chair back and rose, half turning toward the door. Then jumped back, her heart slamming into her throat.

Looming in the doorway of her makeshift office was the shadow of a man. Big. Broad. Powerful. Her mind made the observations in short staccato succession. But it was the gun nestled beneath one muscled bicep that held her attention.

Oh, God. She ripped off the headphones, stumbling a little as she backed away, stopped short by the desk. Her hands searched the surface behind her as she tried to recall if she'd unpacked anything that could be used as a weapon. With a sinking feeling she realized just as quickly that she'd focused on getting her computer and equipment up and running. Her cameras unloaded. Although a knife or pickax would come in handy right now, the most lethal thing on her desk was a bundle of unsharpened pencils.

"You're in the wrong house," she said clearly, as she inched her way along the desk. Her camera tripods were in the corner. Short of heaving the computer monitor at him, they were the heaviest objects in the room. Maybe she could hit him with one and bolt through the doorway.

Maybe he'd shoot her before she lifted a finger.

"Are you drunk? Lost?" She prayed her desperation didn't sound in her voice. Rivers of fear snaked down her spine to pool at the base. He didn't move. Didn't speak. Shrouded in shadows, he appeared only half-human. "You'll have to leave. You don't belong here."

"Now that's real funny." His humorless words could have been chipped from ice. "That's exactly what I was going to say to you."

He flipped the switch and the room was flooded with light. Her concentration abruptly splintered. The music pouring through her headphones had masked his entrance, so he'd gotten her attention the only way he could. On the heels of that realization came another: the light did little to allay her fear.

He was dressed in jeans, a snug navy T-shirt, boots and an attitude. His eyes were very nearly as black as his hair. Penetrating. Merciless. His expression was as unyielding as the sandstone bluffs that dotted the desert.

She'd been to more of the world's trouble spots than she liked to recall. Had photographed wild-eyed fanatics, zealots willing to die for a cause, power-hungry warlords. None of those men had scared her as much as the one standing in front of her. She'd known what motivated them, and the lengths they'd go to get it.

It was impossible to tell what this man was capable of.

Recognition of that fact had her moving again. Gracelessly she stumbled toward the corner, grasped the sturdiest of the tripods and hefted it threateningly. "Get out." Panic morphed abruptly to anger. She'd spent too much time in the last two years being afraid. And she wasn't going to give him that kind of control over her. "Unless you want to be nursing a smashed skull, get the hell out of here. Now."

His gaze lingered on the puny weapon she was wielding, flicked to the corner, then to the heap of camera cases piled next to the desk. Taking two long strides to the computer, he stared hard at the images on the screen.

His voice was as sharp as a rifle shot. "You're Delaney Carson."

The words were couched as an accusation. His glare was condemning. Neither was reassuring enough to make Delaney set down her makeshift weapon. She shifted her stance, readiness in every muscle. "More to the point, who are you? And what are you doing in my house?"

His lips twisted. "You mean my grandfather's house, don't you? Charley Youngblood?"

He didn't look much like the tribal elder who had picked her up at the Tuba City airport that afternoon. But then, that man had at least five decades on the one standing in front of her. That man had been reserved but charming. That man hadn't worn a gun.

"Let's see some ID."

"Grandfather never mentioned that you'd be staying here."

It wasn't an apology. Not even close. It barely qualified as an explanation. The tripod was starting to get heavy, so she repositioned it and repeated firmly, "ID."

His hand went to his hip pocket. Extracting a slim leather case, he flipped it open and held it out to her. She had to inch closer to read the name above the unsmiling picture that was an accurate depiction of the man before her. But it was the gold star below the photo that captured her attention.

"Criminal Investigation?" Giving this man—Joseph Youngblood—a shield and a gun had to be redundant. He exuded threat without either. "What are you investigating?"

"My grandfather never told me he'd be putting you up. I saw the light and thought there might be trouble. It's isolated out here." He tucked away the ID and in one continuous movement reached out to take the tripod away from her. Striding over to the corner, he rested it against the others before returning to survey her from the doorway.

Neither of them spoke. It was all she could do to keep from fidgeting under his impassive stare. Delaney was all too aware of her bare feet, the brief shorts and top she'd changed into after she'd showered. The shirt's narrow straps hadn't allowed for a bra, and that had been fine with her. The temperature had neared one hundred that afternoon, and she hadn't planned on seeing anyone this evening. But now she felt naked, exposed in a way that had her skin tingling and her pulse chugging. She was at a distinct disadvantage, and the sensation was unwelcome.

"Unless you're planning to charge me with unlawfully accepting a place to live, you're done here, aren't you?"

He leaned one shoulder against the door frame, folded his arms across his very impressive chest. "Am I?"

She measured the space between him and the

doorway with her gaze. The only way through was to squeeze by all that hard sinew and smoldering animosity. Deciding to stay put, she backed up to rest a hip against the desk corner. "How'd you get in?"

He held out a key. "We keep a spare outside. You'll want to put it somewhere safe. This place doesn't have more than a standard dead bolt to secure the doors and like I said, it's pretty isolated."

"I like isolated." But she took the key and slipped it into the pocket of her shorts. "I'll be fine."

"There wasn't a vehicle out front. Or in back."

Her gaze narrowed as comprehension dawned. "How long were you lurking around outside before you decided to invite yourself into the house?"

He didn't answer her question, a fact that didn't escape her. "I knocked. But you wouldn't have noticed if I'd driven a truck through the place with those things on." He pursed his lips, twisted them to the side in the direction of her discarded headphones, an act she'd already learned was uniquely Native American. The gesture drew her attention to his mouth, to the chiseled lips and the uncompromising chin, and a crazy little spiral of heat arrowed through her.

Delaney placed her hands on the desk on either side of her hips and clutched the surface, hard. If this was her long-dormant femininity stirring awake, it had lousy timing. And taste in men.

Navajo Nation President Frank Taos had warned her when she'd agreed to this project that some tribal members were opposed to her hiring. It went without saying that Joseph Youngblood was one of them. He couldn't have made it more obvious that he didn't want her here.

"So what are you going to do about that?"

She blinked. "What?"

"You're going to need a vehicle to get around in, aren't you?"

Oh. That. She moistened her lips. "I've got a dealership delivering an SUV tomorrow morning. Don't worry about me. I can take care of myself."

He lifted a brow sardonically. Considering it was the first real emotion she'd read on his face, it was too bad it made her want to smack him.

"Okay, so you waltzed in here unnoticed," she conceded. "But unless you have more keys stashed outside, I should be safe now."

He said nothing, just surveyed her with an implacable stare that had heat crawling across her skin. After a long moment he gave a curt nod. "Lock the door after me." And with a few long strides he was gone, the door closing quietly behind him.

She let out a slow shaky breath. Movements strangely wooden, she lurched to the door to lock it and secure the dead bolt.

She turned back to the small living area. The whole episode had rattled her. She could admit that without feeling weak. But there was a lingering sense of vulnerability that was as unwelcome as the man who'd just left. And that wasn't acceptable at all.

Delaney rubbed her arms with her hands, resolutely

heading back to the office. It wasn't Youngblood's hostility that bothered her. She'd been covering bloody conflicts in countries all over the world for far too long to shy away from one man's displeasure. It was Youngblood himself that gave her pause.

It had been a long time since she'd felt that aware of a man. And given that it was a man she was pretty sure she didn't even like, it was an unwanted complication.

Sitting back down in front of the computer, she tried to focus. There was something to be said for the numbed cocoon in which she'd spent much of the last two years. Something comfortable in a solitary existence free of expectations. She was ready to rejoin the world. She was certain of that. What she was less certain of was her readiness—willingness—to reexperience all the sensations that came with it.

She couldn't identify the individual emotions that had reared up in the last ten minutes. Didn't want to. It was so much safer to wall them off, to keep a distance from feelings that could suck you in, suck you dry.

She typed a command into the computer and waited for a photo to print. Distance was safe. Smart. She could do her job. She could live her life. But she didn't have to give in to that dark tangle of human need that seemed to impose pain far more frequently than pleasure. She hadn't left her self-imposed exile until she'd been damned sure the defenses around her emotions were as stalwart as a fireproof vault.

And she was going to do everything in her power to keep them that way.

Chapter 2

A<small>S</small> Delaney nosed her leased red Jeep down the highway and picked up speed, her spirits lifted accordingly. When she'd woken that morning she'd wanted to dive into work. Instead, she'd forced herself to tend to the drudgery of chores that accompanied her arrival in a new place. Her number one priority yesterday had been getting her office organized and checking her cameras and equipment for possible damage suffered through shipping. But today there had been the inevitable unpacking, and—because she enjoyed regular meals—grocery shopping at Bashas'.

After the reception she'd gotten last night from Youngblood, she'd been a little wary about introducing herself at the store. Although a few of the curious expressions had gone flat and inscrutable, at least none of the locals she'd met today had matched the simmering animosity she'd sensed in Joe Youngblood. She was willing to label that a positive.

It felt good to have a sense of purpose again. She'd set an itinerary of sorts yesterday when Youngblood senior had picked her up at the airport. He wouldn't be available to spend time with her until tomorrow, and she wasn't scheduled to check in with Taos until late this afternoon. Which meant she still had hours left to satisfy a bit of the interest scorching a path through her system.

There would be plenty of occasions to immerse herself in the culture, the people, events and daily life that hummed quietly along on the Navajo reservation. But for the next little while it was the land itself that called to her.

Charley Youngblood had given her a packet, prepared by the council, that included a map of the Navajo Nation. Parts of it were highlighted. From the scrawled note attached, President Taos had had the foresight to receive permission from some property owners to allow Delaney access to their land. She'd been delighted with that discovery and anxious to make use of the consents.

Some would think the area desolate, she mused, setting the cruise after guiltily checking her speedometer. And it *was* barren in spots. Frequent gusts of breeze lifted red dust and then let it settle again over the vast stretches of sand. But every so often the terrain would be interrupted with spectacular rock formations of rosy sandstone, rising majestically skyward. There would be time later to explore Coal Mine Canyon or the mystical Canyon de Chelly. Today she didn't want the disruption of tourists and crowds pressing in around her. There was no shortage of slot canyons and narrows dotting the reservation, and she had a full tank of gas, Norah Jones in stereo and, she hoped, unlimited air-conditioning. She continued to drive.

It was a good hour before it occurred to her that she was much farther north than she'd meant to go. She'd gotten off the main highway and the road she'd taken, although it had started out paved, had turned into little more than a dirt path about a half hour back. But there were some intriguing sandstone cliffs clustered ahead that jutted upward, brooding and massive, from the severe landscape. And if she read her map correctly, she had permission to explore the area.

She pulled over to the side of the road. Taking her Canon SLR out of its case, she selected a zoom lens and screwed it on. She made sure the scenic wide-angle lens was tucked in the case, then slipped the strap over her head, letting it dangle over her shoulder. Hanging the camera strap around her neck, she got out. There were no fences delineating the land from the road. She'd read that many property owners kept sheep, but this spot didn't look appropriate for grazing. It was rocky, with only sparse vegetation.

Watching her footing, she scrambled down the steep incline to get closer. The sheer magnificence of the massive formation was breathtaking. She shot the area from all angles, using the zoom in her approach and quickly growing engrossed in her work. The isolation of the area made it easy to imagine being the first person to stand here thousands of years ago, marveling over the same sight.

As she got closer to the butte she paused long enough to switch lenses before continuing her work. It wasn't until she looked back and saw how small her vehicle appeared in the distance that she realized how far she had come.

She meant only to round the cliffs, placing her between the faces of the two largest formations, before heading back to her vehicle. She ducked her head, intent on removing the specialized lens from the camera when the loud crack reverberated through the air.

Her body reacted before her mind did. Cradling the camera in her arms to protect it, she hit the ground. Logic followed more sluggishly.

Gunfire.

The second shot kicked up red dirt ten feet to her left. The third and fourth were no closer, but neither were they farther away.

She lay frozen against the sunbaked earth, her heart thudding wildly, the sound reverberating in her ears. For an instant past melded with present and a rush of déjà vu burst through her mind with crystal clarity.

The mortar fire that had been a constant backdrop of noise in Baghdad. The crack of a sniper's rifle from the top of the government building across from the outdoor café that had killed the American diplomat she'd been having tea with. The terrific explosion that had torn through the hotel, killing her lover, her friends and colleagues...

The next shot split through the memories and brought her hurtling back to the present. There was no question of who the target was here. She was the only creature in sight. In plain sight, unfortunately.

An occasional saguaro bush dotted the landscape. Some medium-sized rocks. Neither would offer much in the way of cover, but her options were limited.

Force of habit had her protecting the camera as she rolled to her feet, and began running a zigzag pattern back toward her vehicle. She heard the solid sound of a bullet hitting stone and knew the shooter was still there. Still aiming for her. Still missing.

She was unwilling to stick around and discover whether that was due to luck or deliberation.

Delaney moved as fast as she could, dodging around the paltry cover the rocks or bushes afforded as she passed. Another shot sounded. She wondered grimly if it really was farther away or if that was wishful thinking on her part. Her breath rasped in and out of her lungs. The sun was brutal overhead. Sweat snaked rivulets down her skin. The incline was getting steeper as she neared her vehicle. She hadn't realized how sharp the slope was when she'd descended it. She'd been too intent on capturing the primitive beauty of the sandstone cliffs.

As another shot rang out, she found herself wondering if that primitive beauty was going to turn into her death trap.

The pounding of her heart sounded in her ears. Although her thighs ached with exertion, she took the incline at top speed. Finally the vehicle loomed large and comfortingly solid before her. Yanking open the front door she dived inside, keeping her head low, then pulled the door shut behind her. When she started the vehicle the noise of the engine was the most reassuring thing she'd ever heard.

Delaney threw the Jeep into reverse and drove it straight backward, away from the shooter. Away from the cliffs that concealed him. Then she did a Y-turn and headed back to the main road at a speed that was probably not totally safe.

But it was far, far safer than what awaited her back at the cliffs.

"Are we ready for a warrant?" Navajo Tribal Police Captain Jim Tapahe tapped the edge of his pen against the mound of paperwork on his desk. Though Joe saw the man diligently plowing through paperwork day after day, the pile was as much a permanent fixture of the office as the row of battered filing cabinets lining one wall.

"Karen Nez came through for us," Joe replied. "The buy went down exactly where she said it would and we got the pictures." Arnie rose, handed the small bundle of photos to the captain, who began flipping through them.

"And she'll testify that Quintero is her supplier?"

Joe hesitated long enough to have the captain glancing up at him. "She says she will. But she's scared.

I can't guarantee that she won't change her mind if someone gets to her."

Tapahe studied the photos closely, then gave them back to Arnie. "Well, we've got enough to go forward. Hopefully whatever you collect at Quintero's place will be enough to nail him, with or without Nez's testimony. I'll get the request to the judge this afternoon, and I'll ask for a rush on the—"

The intercom on the desk buzzed. "Frank Taos on line one, sir."

Joe and Arnie rose as Tapahe reached for the phone. "I'll let you know as soon as the paperwork comes in," the captain said. Nodding, Joe closed the door after them.

"Think we'll be able to move tonight?"

"I doubt it." They walked toward their desks, and Joe scooped a fast-food wrapper off the top of Arnie's littered desktop, crumpled it and shot it into the wastebasket. "It's already past four. We'd be lucky to get it by tomorrow morning."

"So maybe I'll get home on time. Shock Brenda."

Joe eyed his partner's desk. "Shock me," he suggested. "Clean off your desk first so when we do get that warrant it doesn't get lost in the debris."

"You're a funny guy." Arnie dropped down into his chair. "I have my own method of organization, which you can't hope to understand, much less…"

The captain's door opened. "Youngblood, in here." Joe exchanged a look with his partner before turning to follow Tapahe into his office. The man closed the door and returned to his desk. "That was Navajo Nation

President Taos on the phone. Seems someone took a few shots at that woman the council hired—the one who's writing the book."

A chill trickled down Joe's back. "Delaney Carson."

Tapahe looked down at the notes he'd scribbled and nodded. "That's her. She was out taking pictures when the shots were fired."

Joe had a mental flash of the woman he'd faced off with last night, visibly shaken but wielding a tripod, ready to defend herself against an intruder.

Throat tight, he asked, "Was she hit?"

"No. But Taos is pretty upset. There were plenty who didn't approve of an outsider being hired, and he thinks this might be the work of one of them. He doesn't want any more bad publicity about this project, so we're to get on it right away and report back to him immediately. He asked specifically that you be the one to check it out."

"Me?" Wariness mingled with surprise. "Why me?"

Impatience flickered in the captain's eyes. "Your grandfather is going to be working closely with her, Taos said. She's even staying at one of his houses, right? Seems logical he'd ask for you."

Logical. It was the last word he'd use, given his own feelings about her hiring. Or his reaction to the woman herself.

Tapahe's attention was drifting back toward his paperwork. "Is there a problem?"

Joe smiled grimly. "No problem. I'll check it out and get back to you."

* * *

Delaney reluctantly shut off the water. The house wasn't equipped with air-conditioning and the fans didn't do much more than stir the warm air inside. But there was plenty of cold water, and the pressure was good. The pounding shower had gone a long way to restoring her rattled equilibrium.

She stepped out and dried off briskly. Lying to herself had been one of the habits she'd kicked in the last couple years. So she could admit to the mind-numbing fear that had encased her at the cliffs, even as her mind had gone into survival mode. But greater than the natural fright of the circumstances had been her fear of its aftermath.

But the flashbacks, while present, hadn't left her huddled and shaking, struggling to differentiate between the past and the now. She hadn't had a panic attack or been left with that unquenchable desire to dive into the bottom of a bottle of Absolut.

And that felt like a victory of sorts.

She'd known she was getting stronger, closer to the woman she'd once been. But it was one thing to think it, and another to have that belief put to the test. Someone had tried to kill her. She still shuddered at the thought. But she hadn't broken down and she hadn't given in to the fear that had lived like a sharp-fanged beast in her mind for too long. She was entitled to feel just a little cocky about that.

Securing the towel around herself, she left the bathroom before coming to an abrupt halt, a strangled scream in her throat when her mind registered an intruder. This time, the uninvited man wasn't standing in her office, however, he was lounging on her couch.

As recognition flickered, panic died. "Damn you, Youngblood." She stalked toward him, half-tempted to snatch his gun out of its harness and use it on him. "What is it with you and locked doors? Do they represent some sort of challenge? You can't pass one by without barging in?"

He'd risen at her approach, his mouth opened, but she never gave him a chance to respond. That first startled leap of fear had been elbowed aside by temper. "I can't believe that rules governing civil behavior are so different here that it's considered all right to break into someone else's house whenever you damn well…"

He closed his hand over the finger she was jabbing into his chest. "Maybe we should continue this conversation after you get dressed."

Delaney yanked away from his grasp but didn't step back. "We'll continue it now. What are you doing in my house again?"

"The door was unlocked…"

"The hell it was!" Her interruption had his eyes flaring but she ignored the warning sign and barreled on. "The screen door was latched. That's an unspoken signal the occupant doesn't want people just strolling in." Her sarcastic tone had him tightening his lips.

"If you think that little hook and latch is going to keep anybody out, I guess you just found out otherwise, didn't you? All I had to do was slip a credit card in there and flip it loose."

His words incensed her further. "Normal people don't go around doing that. What do I have to do to keep you from wandering in here at will? Put bars on the windows and retinal scans at the doors?"

Grimly, he ground out, "It isn't me you should be worried about. I'm not the one who shot at you today, am I?"

It was her turn to be silenced. Fury receded, to be replaced by confusion. "How did you know about that?" When she'd called President Taos on her cell, she'd reported the incident to him, and he'd been noticeably upset, assuring her he'd take care of it. Delaney had assumed a police officer would be contacting her. It never occurred to her to expect Youngblood. She hadn't thought a tribal police investigator would deal with routine calls.

When she said as much, Joe's mouth twisted. "Apparently, you aren't considered 'routine.' Taos wants this taken care of before it can become a full-blown incident, with political fallout that could cost him at the next election."

It was impossible to miss the sarcasm in his tone. Pointedly, she looked from him to the now-unlatched front door. "I'd have preferred another officer."

The verbal swipe was lost on him. He no longer seemed to be listening. She followed the direction of his gaze and noticed that the towel had loosened, draping lower across the top of her breasts. She was still covered decently, but the sight reminded her that she was naked but for the towel, hair wet and already probably settling into its usual obnoxious waves.

The realization had her taking a step back. She hated being at a disadvantage around him. Hated the fact that his slow perusal of her form had thousands of tiny little flames flickering to life beneath her skin. She wasn't backing down, but she knew when to beat a strategic retreat. "You can explain later. I'm getting dressed." She turned her back on him and walked quickly toward her bedroom.

Delaney thought she heard him mutter, "Good idea," which only fanned the flames of awareness. He didn't earn any points for somehow turning this around so that *she* was the one embarrassed in her own home.

She pulled on a pair of lightweight khaki capris and a green tank top and slid her feet into matching tennis shoes. Raking her hair into a quick knot, she secured it and in record time joined Joe once again in the living room. He was seated in one of the armchairs.

"I'm sorry if I scared you."

He was a master of taking her by surprise. She may have deserved an apology, but she hadn't expected to get it. By offering one so freely, he defused a fraction of her anger, which made her slightly uneasy. She took a stance behind the couch to face him, as he continued.

"I did knock. Stood out on the porch for about fifteen minutes, as a matter of fact. When pounding on the door didn't get your attention I thought maybe something was wrong."

She folded her arms across her chest. "I was taking a shower."

His eyes glinted. "I didn't know that until I was inside, did I?"

She considered the excuse for a moment and then shook her head. "Flimsy, Youngblood. Very flimsy. I can't imagine breaking into your house in a similar situation."

He was beginning to look annoyed. Under the circumstances, she was glad. Any reaction from him was better than the implacable expression he usually wore. "Someone shot at you. It wasn't unreasonable to consider, when you didn't answer, that maybe that same someone had shown up to finish the job."

She blinked. That was a little scenario she hadn't thought of. Since her knees felt a little shaky, she leaned against the couch. "I think the shots were fired to scare me off. To get me away from the area I was exploring."

"Might have been," he agreed. "Or it could have been someone recognized you and took the opportunity to express displeasure at your being on the reservation. Did you see anyone?" When she shook her head, he pressed, "Did you notice any other vehicles? Evidence that people had been using the area?"

Although she shook her head again, he didn't relent, leading her through the entire sequence of events with a thoroughness that wasn't lost on her. "What about the pictures you took?"

"How do you know I was taking pictures?"

"Another logical assumption." His voice was dry. "It's what you do, right? And you said you'd wanted some shots of the cliffs. Maybe we'll see something in one of them that will give us a clue to the identity of the shooter. Or the reason he wanted you out of there."

"I haven't downloaded the pictures yet. I've been sort of busy."

He nodded. "Okay, we'll deal with that later. In the meantime, there's plenty of daylight left. Why don't you take me back to where it happened."

She stared at him, nonplussed. Although his words had been couched as a suggestion, she knew him well enough to know there had been an order hidden in there somewhere.

"I could loan you the map I used, if you promised to return it," she said grudgingly. "You could go check it out...."

"No need," he said, heading toward the door. "You're coming with me. We'll take my Jeep."

Joe took his eyes off the road long enough to slide a look at the silent woman in the seat beside him. He'd had hostile witnesses more talkative.

Delaney's reluctance to accompany him had been obvious. But he wasn't going to set off on a possible wild-goose chase when she could just as easily direct him herself. Despite the map, she couldn't describe where it had happened. She'd need landmarks to find the exact area again.

The sun was still bright. Heat waves shimmered off the highway. He reached up to the visor, slid his sunglasses out from their holder and put them on. He wasn't thrilled about spending the next few hours in her company, either. Especially when it was all too easy to imagine her in the brief yellow towel that had left enough bared skin to have his hormones flickering to life.

His mouth thinned. Hormones were primitive things, unhindered by judgment or good sense. All his body's response really meant was that it had been too long since he'd last gotten laid. It had been hard to summon interest, or much else, since Heather had taken off with Jonny.

But in one of life's cruel little ironies, *interest*, and a lot more, was raised by this woman. She was the last type of female he'd ever consider getting involved with. She was another *belagana*, like his ex, and his failed marriage had taught him that non-Navajos could never understand the link he had to this place, to the land where his ancestors had lived.

Logic, however, played a poor second to lust. None of those reasons mattered, because permanency was the last thing he was looking for. They didn't have to like each other for Joe to act on the heat that flared in the pit of his belly whenever he thought of Delaney. Wild, hot, mind-numbing sex didn't have to have a damn thing to do with the brain.

Resolutely, he shoved aside the wayward thoughts. He'd never been a man to be controlled by the area south of his belt. Nor did he seek out needless complications, which Delaney Carson had written all over her.

She leaned forward and started fiddling with the rearview mirror.

"What are you doing?"

"Changing the temperature button to the one marked compass." She sat back. "This afternoon I didn't end up where I was originally heading, but I know the directions I went. Pretty much."

"Around here we call that lost."

"Do you?" She aimed a dazzling smile at him. "I call it differently located."

That smile hit him square in the chest with the force of a fast right jab. Any other woman would still be shaky and maybe a bit hysterical after what she'd been through. She shouldn't be humorous, displaying an unmistakable charm that made him stop and wonder if there was more to her than he'd considered earlier.

And the fact that he did wonder irritated the hell out of him.

"Turn north on Highway 89," she said.

He slowed, and turned as she requested. "How'd you happen to get lost if you were on the highway?"

"This isn't the way I came, but I ended up on this road on the way back. Anyway, it was when I got off the main roads that I wound up…somewhere other than where I'd intended."

It was safer to retreat behind a professional mask. "It'd be wise to take a guide with you the next time you get the urge to go exploring. A person can die of heatstroke pretty rapidly in this climate. Not to mention the chance of happening on a poisonous snake, scorpion or black widow."

Her smile faded and she turned back to the window. "I'm aware of the dangers. I took the precaution of packing a survival kit for my vehicle."

"If one of those shots had found its mark, you wouldn't have had the chance to get back to the Jeep for the kit," he replied grimly. "No one would have known where you were. Chances are you'd have died out there and it would have taken days for someone to find your body."

"Nice thought," she muttered, rubbing her arms. "You'll be happy to know the Navajo Tribal Council has arranged to place a guide at my disposal." She craned her neck to look out the window. "I'm not inexperienced in traveling in remote places, but this isn't exactly Afghanistan or Iraq. There, women weren't safe alone in public, so obviously I was never unescorted. Foreign journalists are obvious targets for kidnapping. Indonesia was just as volatile."

Her words had him surveying her more carefully. He'd heard something of her background, but hadn't familiarized himself with the details. "So why'd you keep going to those kinds of places?" Some people were adrenaline junkies. He could understand that. Police departments had their share.

Her face swung to his, genuine surprise in her expression. "For the stories, of course. How would you get your news about what's happening outside our country if people like me didn't report it?"

The reasonableness of her response was lost on him. "But why *you?* What was there about the job that made you take the kind of risks you did, day after day, for years?"

She seemed to be searching for words. "My father is a painter," she said finally. "He makes a living with his portraits, but his love is the stills. I used to watch him mix his paints when I was little. He'd spend hours getting just the right shade of blue and I couldn't understand that. Sky is blue. Just choose blue and get on with it, right? But he used to say, 'the impact lies in the shade I use.'"

She pushed her glasses on top of her head, and Joe found himself distracted by her eyes, with their odd, exotic slant and curious wash of color. He couldn't recall ever seeing that gray-green hue before, with the startling band of gold around the irises.

And he couldn't recall the last time he'd bothered to analyze a woman's eye color.

"Photography was my first love," Delaney was saying. "I took journalism classes just so I could do something with it, but quickly figured out I got hooked on the story. Not only what happened, but why. Your job, it's more cut and dried, isn't it? Someone does something to someone and you find out who did it. Make them pay. But truth isn't always black and white."

"That's what most of my suspects would say," he replied wryly.

"I've seen the devastation, the poverty in some of those countries, the results of primitive governments and war. But the story, the truth, varies depending on whose eyes I'm telling the story through. In a time when news can be slanted to suit political purposes, it's even more important to show all sides. That's what my photos do. Put tangibles, faces to the news. Because the impact lies in the pictures I use."

He heard the passion in her voice, and could appreciate the enthusiasm she had for her job, even if he couldn't fully understand what drew her to it. But then, most people didn't get why he'd chosen investigative work, when his college degree would have qualified him for a number of higher-paying occupations. People were lucky to feel that kind of commitment to any job. When they did, it was impossible to imagine doing anything else.

"I got the feeling from your grandfather yesterday that you and he are close."

The shift in conversation caught him by surprise. "Yes."

"But you don't approve of my being here. Of his cooperation on this project."

He kept his voice carefully neutral. "Did I say that?"

"Your reaction yesterday did. You didn't exactly roll out the welcome mat when you figured out who I was." When he remained silent, she prodded, "Has your difference of opinion caused problems between you and your grandfather? Because I wouldn't want…"

"My relationship with my grandfather is none of your business," he said succinctly. He didn't need her reminder that he hadn't yet spoken to the older man, hadn't smoothed out the friction that had risen between them in the last week or so. "We aren't two of the faces for you to add to your project. Our personal lives are off-limits."

"Really." She twisted in the seat to glare at him. "So it's only questions about me that are fair game." She nodded, as if in understanding. "Be sure and write these rules down for me so I don't make the mistake of believing you're capable of rational conversation."

She couldn't make him feel small. Not about this. "We were having a rational conversation."

"Wrong. Since you were the only one allowed to ask questions, it was more of an interrogation. But don't worry. The boundaries are clearly marked. I caught that. Take a right up here."

He almost missed the direction, couched as it was with sarcasm. He took the corner a little fast and she slapped a hand on the dash to brace herself. But she didn't say anything else. As a matter of fact, she lapsed into the same silence she'd kept earlier, and this time he wasn't stupid enough to try to get her talking.

Tension all but crackled in the interior of the vehicle. Delaney spoke only to give him a direction to take. When she did, he could almost scrape the ice off her words.

That was okay. He gripped the wheel with both hands on the rough, uneven dirt road they'd taken. Ice was good. It would help maintain a distance between them that would defuse the heat.

He had the feeling he was going to need all the help he could get.

Chapter 3

"This is the place." If revisiting the spot she'd been shot at bothered Delaney, it didn't show in her voice.

"You're sure?" Joe was already slowing down, looking in the direction she pointed. The collection of rose-colored sandstone buttes and jagged spears of rock jutting skyward clustered around steep massive cliffs of the same color.

"There's a sort of road coming up. Probably went a quarter mile on it before I parked." Her head swung toward him when he stopped the vehicle. "Don't you want to get closer?"

"Not without trying to see if whoever took those shots at you is still around." He unbuckled his seat belt and reached into the back seat for the binoculars he'd brought along. Withdrawing the high-powered glasses from the case, he scanned the area carefully. There was no sign of anyone. But then, the bluffs provided ample protection for a person who wanted to stay out of sight.

His 9 mm pistol wasn't going to be much use in this situation so he unbuckled his holster, folded it around the gun and put it in the glove compartment. Then he slipped the strap of the binoculars over his head, got out of the SUV and opened the back door. He saw Delaney's brows rise over the top of her sunglasses when he took the rifle out of its rack and quickly loaded it.

"I'd think the person who fired those shots at me would be long gone."

"You're probably right, but in case he isn't, I like my odds better this way." He shut the back door and ducked his head into the driver's side door he'd left open. "Which way did you approach the cliffs?"

"I parked parallel to that first butte." She pointed. "After taking some pictures, I wanted to get closer. I was going to go around and between the two largest formations toward the car. I didn't round them before the first shot was fired."

Grimly, Joe studied the area. Between the formations and where she'd parked, there was very little in the way of cover. She'd practically been a sitting duck. It made him suspect that the shots hadn't been meant to hit her. Unless the person had been an incompetent marksman, there was no way he would miss.

Whether she'd been a real target or just meant to be frightened off, she still could have been caught by a bullet. And he found himself hoping that whoever had tried it was still around here somewhere. He wouldn't mind dealing with him himself.

"Stay here," he ordered, as Delaney started to get out of the SUV.

"Like hell." She jumped out and slammed the door shut.

He rounded the hood of the vehicle and blocked her path. "Don't think I won't use handcuffs if I have to."

"You could try," she said coolly, hands on her hips. "I wouldn't make it easy."

"Tell me something I don't know," he muttered. "Let me check things out. If there's trouble, I don't need to be worrying about you presenting another possible target."

"You wouldn't have to worry about me if I were armed. I could carry your revolver."

Ice filled his veins. "The idea of arming you scares me worse than possibly walking into a trap. Just stay here, all right? The guy is probably long gone. If you see me wave, go ahead and pull the car around to where you parked yesterday."

Delaney folded her arms across her chest and glared at him. "And what do you want me to do if someone starts shooting at you?"

"Use the radio to alert dispatch." He strode away before she could state the obvious. Even provided they could find the location from her directions, it would be too late for help to arrive in time.

It was probably a moot point in any case. The department-issued radios were spotty at best in the more remote areas of the Rez. If there was someone still hiding among the cliffs, Joe was probably on his own.

He strode rapidly toward the bluffs, frequently raising the binoculars and scanning the area. Still no sign of anyone. If the shooter had a brain in his head, he'd have cleared out after firing those shots.

He turned in the direction he'd come. The Jeep was a half mile in the distance and with the glasses he could easily make out Delaney, her expression impatient. The sight had something in him lightening.

It was half-surprising that she'd remained there as ordered. A woman wasn't as successful as she was in her line of work by being a passive bystander. When it came to reporting the world news from global trouble spots, photojournalism was still very much a man's world.

Which didn't explain what had kept her traveling from one war-torn country after another. The reason she'd offered had only whetted his curiosity and that wouldn't do at all. He could ill afford to be distracted by anything these days, least of all a woman.

Especially *this* woman.

Because caution was ingrained in him, he approached in a zigzag, taking what cover he could behind rocks or scraggly bushes. The place was still, the sun searing through the bright blue sky even as it began its descent toward the horizon. A hawk did a lazy swoop from atop the far cliff, on the hunt to feed the hungry mouths back at its nest.

He was even with the first bluff now, and the outcrop of smaller rocks was thicker here. His pace quickened.

He wanted plenty of time to look around before heading back to Tuba City. They had a couple more hours of daylight, and he'd need all of it to do a thorough...

The sound of an engine split through the quiet like a siren at midnight. Joe ran in a crouch toward the sound, thumbing off the rifle's safety as he went. As he rounded the foot of the first rosy cliff, he had to jump backward to avoid being run over.

The ATV leaped out at him, the driver bent low over the handlebars. The man atop it wore a ball cap low, and a shocked expression.

Joe rose and sighted the rifle in one smooth move. "Tribal Police," he called out. "Stop the vehicle."

In answer, the driver gunned the motor and reached beneath his shirt. Joe ducked behind some rocks as the first shot rang out. He returned fire, aiming for the rear tires on the ATV. But the driver was quickly pulling farther away.

Joe squeezed off a rapid sequence of shots and then dived as the driver returned fire. There was little chance of hitting the man even had Joe been trying. The vehicle was packed with boxes and bags secured to the ATV in a precarious pile.

Red dirt swirled in the vehicle's trail. Joe ran in its path, sighted and fired again. He squinted through the cloud of dust and saw the ATV veer, hit a rock. Certain he'd struck a tire, he ran faster. But the driver righted the vehicle, and roared off, the packages teetering unsteadily.

Biting back a curse, Joe stopped, wiping his forehead with the back of one arm. He might have had a chance of catching the vehicle if he'd had the Jeep here, but on foot he was...

The Jeep. He sent a wary glance at the space between the cliffs and jogged around the closest bluff, staying close to the rocks. He wasn't at all surprised to find the spot where he'd left Delaney and the Jeep obscured by puffs of dust. When she heard the shots she must have taken the opportunity to get closer, despite his directions otherwise.

Heaving a sigh, he brushed off his jeans and turned back to the wide clearing between the two bluffs. Using the binoculars he scanned the face of both cliffs, noting the numerous slotlike openings. Plenty of caves in a place like this. Although there was no sign of more vehicles, there were plenty of tire tracks indicating several had been here earlier.

Keeping the rifle ready, he headed toward a good-size opening in the cliff face nearby. When he saw Delaney round the bluff and start toward him, his mouth flattened. He shouldn't have expected otherwise, but was it so damn difficult for her to follow a simple instruction?

In the next instant, Joe saw what she carried and anger replaced frustration. Keeping a wary eye on the area around them, he waited for her to reach him before biting out, "What'd I tell you about touching my gun?"

The revolver looked totally out of place in the hand of a woman wearing cropped pants and a top the color of sour apples. But then, her expression looked out of place, too. Her face was settled in a taut, grim mask, and he had an instant understanding of how she had survived in the world's trouble spots.

"I believe you said something to the effect that if someone tried to blow your head off, you'd be most appreciative of a little help."

He snorted, reached for the weapon. Not surprisingly, she stepped out of his reach.

"I'm no marksman, but I know how to release the safety and fire. I've even been known to hit something, now and again."

"And the flashlight?" She carried his heavy Maglite from the Jeep in her free hand.

She looked down at it. "It's pretty heavy. If I ran out of ammo I figured it'd make a good club."

He studied her for a moment, reevaluating. That she wasn't a woman to stay tucked safely away while the action was going down was growing more clear by the minute. He held out his hand, waiting. His jaw tightened when, rather than handing over the gun, she slapped the flashlight in his outstretched palm. He couldn't see her eyes behind those damn shades, but he knew they'd be mutinous.

"You check out the caves and I'll keep watch outside."

The suggestion had merit, but that didn't lessen his irritation. He tucked the flashlight under one arm, took off the binoculars, and held them out to her, the strap hanging over one crooked finger. "Take these to that cluster of rocks over there. Call out if you see anything at all. And try not to shoot off any of your body parts. Or mine."

Turning, he headed into the nearest opening in the

cliff wall. He could just make out her muttered, "Don't worry, I happen to be quite attached to *my* body parts," and he swallowed the retort that rose to his lips.

Because given half a chance, he had a feeling he could get quite attached to them, too.

The first cave was barely deserving of the name. He had to crawl inside and the sweep of the beam from his flashlight told him that it didn't get any more inviting. To humans, at least.

Some openings in the cliff face were merely good-sized cracks. Others, he discovered, were large enough to provide shelter to any number of four-legged or slithering creatures, none of which he was particularly interested in meeting up with. Given the sheerness of the cliff, he didn't think he needed to worry about the openings above him. There was no visible way to reach them.

After he'd done a quick check of one bluff, he repeated the search on the one opposite. And it was there that he hit pay dirt. Hidden behind two twin rock spires was a cave at ground level. He shone the beam of the flashlight inside it, found it deserted. To avoid a major concussion, he had to duck to step in, but once he'd entered two or three feet, he could stand easily.

It was obvious that someone had been here before him, and left in a hurry. There were kerosene lanterns placed at regular intervals along the cave floor against the walls. The opening was fairly deep; it meandered back through the bluff for at least fifty feet. At one point it widened to an area approximately half that size, and here he found more lanterns, piles of blankets and a heap of empty unmarked cardboard boxes.

A bat swooped toward his head, and Joe dodged, using the flashlight to explore the extent of the cave. It ended against a rough rock wall, and in the corner he found cartons of bottled water, dried packaged food and litter a foot deep. He kicked through the trash, which seemed to consist mostly of food wrappers, empty water bottles and cigarette butts.

He doubled back, switching off the flashlight when he hit the opening again. Blinking rapidly, he ducked out of the cave into the sunlight.

"What'd you find?"

Delaney's tone was impatient, but at least she'd stayed put this time. She stepped out from the rocks toward him.

"Someone has been here. Several someones." He looked up at the sky, gauged how much sunlight he had left.

"What about that guy who fired at you? Any chance you could follow his tracks and see where he went?"

"Sure, if you happened to bring an ATV along with you," he said with mock politeness.

Her chin angled. "You don't have to get snippy. A Jeep can go off road."

Snippy? He tried to remember if he'd ever had the word applied to him before. He didn't think so. He was pretty sure he would have remembered it. "The Jeep may do cross-country for a while," he allowed, "but it's not going to be much use where the terrain gets rockier.

The earth is too hard in the desert to leave tracks." Joe figured he had less than an hour's worth of sunlight left. Not enough time to try and trail the guy, even if it had been possible.

He went to where the space widened between the two formations, and crouched down to study the ground. The earth was dusty here, crisscrossed with tire tracks. He was aware when Delaney stopped her bored fidgeting and wandered off, but he let her go. The danger here had passed. She'd be safe enough.

Dusk was settling in before he finally rose again, satisfied. At some time there had been at least two ATVs and a truck here.

One set of tracks had a wider wheelbase than an SUV or a pickup. A utility van, maybe? One of the tire marks had an odd tread that didn't match any of the others.

Joe looked around, but didn't see Delaney. Rising, he jogged back to the Jeep and got his investigative kit. Returning, he found the clearest print of the track and took several pictures of the distinctive tread. Then he measured the front and back tire track depth and width and jotted down his findings in his notebook. Noting Delaney was still nowhere in sight, he put down the flashlight and camera, retrieved the rifle and set out after her.

He could see her once he rounded the edge of the sandstone cliff, still a couple hundred yards away. Narrowing his eyes, he noted she had a cardboard box tucked under one arm.

Joe jogged up to meet her. "Funny time to go shopping."

She slapped her free hand to her heart, staggered in feigned shock. "A joke from Joe Youngblood? Will wonders never cease?"

"I joke," he replied, affronted.

"Sarcasm doesn't count. Here." She thrust the dusty box at him. "I think this fell off that ATV. One of its tires must have blown. I saw pieces of rubber. But this is the only parcel I found."

He ripped open the tape holding the flaps shut. Peering inside, he experienced a quick jolt of excitement.

Syringes. Still encased in their original plastic packaging.

She voiced his inner question. "What would he have been doing with a box of syringes?"

"Probably nothing legal." He took the box from her and headed back to the bluffs. She fell into step beside him. "Which explains why they wanted to keep you out of here."

"They?"

"There's been a lot of activity here recently. I don't know what kind of operation you stumbled on, but whatever it was, someone went to a lot of pains to hide it."

"So good work, Delaney, on leading me back here," she said in a painfully bad imitation of his voice. "Say, did I remember to congratulate you on finding that box? I didn't? Well, gee, I guess that makes me a great big…"

"Good job." His lips twitched, but he wouldn't let himself smile. No use encouraging her. "I need to take another look inside that cave before we leave. I didn't see any used syringes in there, but there's plenty of litter. I may have missed something."

Delaney followed him to the entrance of the cave, then looked around, prepared to wait. Joe set the box and rifle down, then in one motion rose and swiped the gun she still held in her hand.

"Hey!"

Ignoring her protest, he shoved the gun in the waist-band of his jeans. "I prefer to keep track of all the weapons myself. Call me paranoid."

"That's not the first adjective that springs to mind."

He gave her a hard look, but said only, "I won't be long. Don't wander off."

His orders were starting to wear thin. "Maybe you'd like to tether me to one of the rocks," she suggested politely. But when he disappeared into the cave without responding, she sighed, scanned the ground carefully and then sat down. She'd known spending any amount of time in his presence was going to be a strain, but it was probably better this way. When she was thinking of how much he annoyed her she wasn't considering the way his jeans hugged his narrow hips, or the inverted V made by shoulders tapering to waist.

Much.

He'd been inside about five minutes when he called out, "Delaney. Come in here a minute, will you?"

She looked up from the drawing she'd been making with her index finger on the sandy ground. "What?"

His voice was more impatient now. Imagine that. "I need you to come hold this light."

Staring blankly at the entrance of the cave, she swallowed hard. "In…there?"

No way. Though her body remained frozen in place, her mind was scrambling for safety. Absolutely not. A cave was closed. Confined. The walls would press in. The air would get scarce.

As if oxygen were already in short supply, she hauled a greedy gulp of it into her lungs as she struggled to her feet. Her brain shouted *Run!* Still she didn't move. Couldn't.

Joe reappeared in the cave's entrance. "What's the matter? You aren't afraid of bats, are you? Because there aren't that many of them. The activity scared them off."

She shook her head, unable to speak.

"Well then, come on."

It was worse, ten times worse with him standing there staring at her. Delaney struggled to keep her face expressionless. To keep the panic that was sprinting up her spine from showing. A man like him could never understand. Had Joe Youngblood ever been afraid of anything? Doubtful. Fear made you weak, and she couldn't imagine him ever feeling weakness.

Which made her doubly reluctant to show it in front of him.

She took a step forward, half-surprised when her foot moved. Another step. Then another. She was even with the entrance of the cave now, and its opening threatened, like a toothless mouth ready to swallow her whole. She stopped next to him, took the flashlight he handed her, then watched him retreat into the near darkness.

Don't think about it. Just do it.

Some post-traumatic stress therapists recommended just this sort of thing, she recalled as she inched farther and farther into the cave. A desensitization experience, under safe conditions, could lay fears to rest for good. And this was safe. Perfectly safe.

She looked over her shoulder. The entrance was still there, the low dusk light spilling inside. There was an escape route. It was all right. She'd be all right.

"I need the light over here."

Delaney followed his voice, trying to ignore the shadows crowding in, surrounding her. She concentrated on the beam of the flashlight before her. The darkness couldn't engulf her as long as the light held out. Surely they wouldn't be in here long enough for the flashlight battery to die.

Joe gripped her shoulders and guided her to the position he wanted, seeming not to notice the stiffness in her limbs. "Point the light at the center of the floor here." He crouched down, began stacking up empty cartons then moving them quickly out of the way. "The guy on the ATV must have cleared all those boxes out of here, but I have to wonder why. At some point they had a truck out there. Why couldn't they have used it to haul stuff?"

"A truck?" Since his words offered a distraction, she seized on them. "Maybe there was something large stored in here that they took away."

Joe finished stacking all the bigger empty cartons and bent to sift through the remaining litter on the floor. "More than likely it would have needed to be dismantled before hauling it out of here. You couldn't manipulate something of any size around those rocks out front."

There was a chill in the air, she was almost certain of it. Surely it came from the cool rocks and not from her sweat-slicked skin. She could feel the blood pounding in her veins, and realized with a start that she was panting. The thin tether she had on her control was slipping.

Joe was saying something, his usual expressionless voice holding a note of excitement, but she couldn't concentrate on his words. The inner chamber of the cave was shrinking, the walls moving in on them with sly sliding movements. The beam highlighting Joe shook in her fingers. She gripped it more tightly, but couldn't hold it steady.

The entrance is still there. There's a way out. I can just walk out.

But she couldn't stop herself from looking over her shoulder, just to be sure. All she could see was the pile of rubbish Joe had stacked.

Delaney stumbled back, straining to see around the pile. In the dim recesses of her mind she knew the entrance was present. It was only feet away. But the path to escape was blocked. It was blocked.

Emotion abruptly overcame reason. She bolted. The flashlight released from her numbed fingers, bounced on the hard cave floor and switched off, throwing the interior into complete darkness. She crashed through the makeshift barricade, stumbling over a carton, nearly falling. But she didn't stop her forward motion toward the entrance. Toward air. Toward freedom.

She burst out of the cave with dizzying speed, tripped over a rock, went sprawling. Her fall drove the breath from her chest and she lay there, lungs heaving, feeling the still-warm air chase the chill from her skin.

It was long moments before she could drag herself upright, draw up her knees and rest her forehead against them. Slowly, panic receded, to be replaced by all-too-familiar symptoms. Her head was pounding in the aftermath of the episode, her body weak. Dizzy. It was the height of irony that only hours earlier she'd been congratulating herself for having conquered the panic. For having found her strength again.

Had she really thought the fears had been driven away? They had only been hiding, waiting until she let her guard down before rushing in to ambush her again. The realization was bitter.

But more bitter by far was finally raising her head, looking up to see Joe Youngblood gazing down at her, with something suspiciously close to pity on his face.

Chapter 4

Captain Tapahe stared at the used syringe in the plastic evidence bag Joe held, his face creased in thought. "It might have been a lucky break for us that Carson stumbled upon the area. If it's as remote as you say, chances are we never would have known anything was going on there."

"Once we get this syringe back from the lab we'll have a better idea just what kind of operation it was." Meaningfully he waved the bag at his captain. "Just how long do you think we'll have to wait for results?"

At Tapahe's hesitation, Joe felt a familiar frustration. The Navajo Tribal Police was hopelessly underfunded. There wasn't enough money to regularly update basic equipment, much less purchase new expensive lab facilities. Most of their forensic evidence was sent off the reservation, to languish at the state crime lab for weeks or longer.

"It's not like this ties in with any of our open cases," the captain began.

"We can't know that until the tests are completed," Joe argued. He hooked a chair with a backward swipe of his ankle and dragged it over to sink into it. The late nights spent on the drug case were beginning to wear on him, coupled as they were by lack of sleep, which had begun to elude him at precisely the same time his ex had decided to run off to Window Rock with his son. "They might find traces of crystal ice in the syringe."

Tapahe nodded. "We'll send it in. I just can't flag it as high priority at this point. That doesn't mean we won't still get the results eventually."

Eventually. Joe swallowed his irritation. Eventually usually meant after a case had gone to trial. He wasn't going to be able to depend on lab results to help determine what had been going on at that cave site.

"I got something else." He showed the captain the photos he'd taken of the tire tracks. "I spent a couple hours on the computer trying to match it against the tire manufacturers' tire tread images, with no luck. I've never seen anything like it before."

Tapahe studied it. "Looks like a Mexican recap, to me. I did a stint on Border Patrol when I was starting out. I think they still do these in some places down there. You salvage a worn-out tire by replacing the original tread with new rubber. They sort of melt it on, pressing a tread into it when the rubber is still soft."

"Mexico, huh?" Joe looked at the photo with renewed interest. The crystal ice that had started showing up on Navajo Nation lands was thought to come from there. It was far more pure and lethal than the meth manufactured in the homemade labs in remote areas on the reservation. "I've got a friend on Border Patrol. I think I'll give him a call."

"Let me know if you get something. In the meantime—" Tapahe cast a look at the clock on the wall "—I better get back to President Taos. He'll be reassured to hear that the person shooting at Carson probably wasn't expressing a statement on the council's decision to hire a non-Navajo for their book project."

At the man's dry tone it struck Joe that the captain had frustrations of his own. The difference was, his came in the form of bureaucrats and paperwork.

Joe rose. All things considered, he'd take his daily annoyances over those of his superior any day. "I'll let you get to that." The mention of Delaney had him edgy. She'd been silent all the way home. Not the kind of silence that had followed their argument on the trip to the bluffs. No, this time instead of frost there had been misery, real and palpable. He'd wanted to say something to break through it. But he recognized the tilt to her chin, her brittle air and knew instinctively that anything he could have said would have worsened the situation. It hadn't made him feel any better watching her stride unsteadily from the Jeep to the house.

He knew what it was to be alone. But he didn't think

he'd seen anyone look as solitary as Delaney had as she'd slipped up those steps and shut the door on him and the rest of the world.

"Search warrant should be here first thing in the morning," Tapahe said. He was already punching the president's number into the phone.

"We'll be ready."

Going to his desk, Joe rummaged through the drawers until he found a small black address book. He and Bernie Silversmith had graduated high school together. They still sometimes got together when the man came back to town to visit family.

Checking the time, he called Bernie at home. The sound of his friend's voice when he answered brought a smile to Joe's lips. "Bernie. You back at work yet or are you still milking what's left of your medical leave?"

"Youngblood? Let me tell you, pal, you can't rush healing. A hernia is nothing to mess around with."

"And what was it that gave you that hernia, again?" Joe wondered aloud. "Lifting all those crates of Twinkies?"

Bernie made a derisive sound and invited Joe to do the anatomically impossible. "I go back tomorrow, as a matter of fact. Against doctor's orders, I'll have you know. It was a major operation."

"Listen, I have something I want to run by you." He described the tread he'd seen at the cave site. "My captain called it a Mexican 'recap.' That sound familiar to you?"

"Sure." The man's shrug sounded in his voice. "We see them from time to time. If you want to fax me the picture and the track dimensions, I'll take it to work, fax it to the other offices. Maybe it will ring a bell with one of the officers." He reeled off the fax number and Joe fumbled for a pen to write it down.

There was a moment of silence, before his friend said awkwardly, "So how are you doing, Joe? I mean I heard the divorce is final and all."

Stomach tightening, Joe twirled the pen in his fingers. "I'm okay." Sympathy wasn't any easier to take, he'd discovered, for being well-meant.

"Yeah? Well, good. Good. Next time I'm up to see the family, I'll stop in. It's been a while."

"You do that. Bring me a Twinkie when you do." His friend's fondness for the treats was a running joke between them. Bernie made another cheerfully rude suggestion and Joe laughed, hung up.

He jotted down the measurements he'd taken of the tracks onto the clearest picture of them and crossed the room to feed it into the fax machine for Bernie. Then, stealing a look at his watch, he winced. Too late to go see his grandfather. With the exception of Monday nights, the man went to bed early and rose before dawn. Joe would have to put it off another day, and the guilt was beginning to eat at him. Charley Youngblood had raised him, and despite the older man's traditional ways, they were close. Respect for elders was a trait instilled in his culture, and his remorse over this disagreement was growing with every day that passed.

The thought of home wasn't inviting. He was still

restless, from thoughts of the arrest they'd make tomorrow and the discovery he'd made today with Delaney.

Delaney. Bernie would probably be surprised to know that it wasn't thoughts of his ex that disturbed his concentration these days, but thoughts of a near stranger. After the hours he'd spent with her he had more questions than ever about the woman, questions she'd made quite clear she was tired of answering.

Without conscious decision he went back to the computer and brought up a search engine.

He shouldn't have come.

Joe stood on the porch of Charley's rental property and knocked again on the open screen door, knowing it was a mistake. He'd had no intention of coming here. Had given himself half a dozen excellent reasons not to. Yet here he was, peering into the dimly lit house looking for a woman who wouldn't welcome his presence. Hell, she'd probably gone to sleep hours ago.

He rejected that thought as it occurred. Given the last sight he'd had of Delaney, sleep was the last thing she'd seek. And now that he had a little understanding of what she'd gone through today, sleep would elude him as well until he assured himself that she was all right.

So here he was, a man unused to offering comfort, looking for a woman probably in need of it. He couldn't imagine a more stupid move.

He almost convinced himself to leave. It was late. Past the time most people would be in bed. But Delaney wasn't in bed. There was a dim light shining in the kitchen and from where he stood he could see the shadow of her sitting at the table, head down.

Alone. His mind flashed back to hours earlier when he'd noted the solitary air she wore, like a woman so used to the feeling that she didn't even notice its weight anymore. And he knew he wasn't going to leave. Just as he knew he was going to regret coming.

Joe reached out, tried the door, unsurprised to find it open. Soundlessly he let it close behind him, walked to the kitchen doorway. She didn't look up.

"I don't want you here." Her voice was flat. Devoid of expression.

"I know."

"Leave."

He folded his arms and leaned a shoulder against the doorjamb. "No."

"You could top off my day and arrest me." She nodded to the bottle of vodka placed precisely in the center of the table before her. "Alcohol of any kind is strictly prohibited on the reservation, isn't it? The seal's been cracked."

She turned to look at him, and held out her hands, wrists together. "Gonna cuff me, Youngblood? Throw me in the drunk tank?" There was mockery in her voice, but he knew it wasn't aimed at him. He would have preferred it if it were.

"I'd hate to have to make another trip into town." She wasn't drunk, he noted. And although the seal on the bottle was cracked, it looked full, or nearly so. Which didn't explain why she'd been sitting in the near dark staring at the bottle as if it held all the answers she sought.

Or the oblivion she craved.

"You should have told me. Today. At the cave." She just stared at him, making it difficult to string together a logical sentence. "You didn't have to go in there. I would never have expected you to if I'd known."

She looked away. "Just a little claustrophobia. Nothing to tell, really."

It burned, more than it should have, that she lied to him. He could understand the need to show strength rather than weakness to a man she had no reason to trust. But the horrific news stories he'd read on the Internet made the offhand manner she attempted a travesty. Buried alive for more than two days with seventy-one corpses. It was a wonder she'd still been coherent after running from the cave.

It was a wonder she'd gone in to begin with.

Silence stretched, long enough to have her glancing at him again. What she saw in his eyes had her swallowing hard. "Did a little research tonight, did you?"

"I didn't think you would tell me." Didn't think he had a right to ask.

Pushing back from the table, she spread her arms wide. "Are you kidding me? My life's an open book. Well, for a year or so there it was an open bottle, but..." Her mouth twisted. "Didn't find that in the news stories, did you? Did the press leave out a few details? Do yóu have a couple more questions to round out your profile of me?"

Her tone was goading, but that wasn't the reason for the sudden flare of temper igniting in his chest. "You

shouldn't have gone inside today. What was the point?
You had nothing to prove, not to me."

Her mouth twisted. "Maybe I had something to
prove to myself, did you ever think of that?"

Comprehension slammed into him. No, he hadn't
thought of that, but he should have. He knew all about
testing himself, forcing himself back into situations
he'd prefer to avoid. At least professionally. In his
personal life, once burned, he steered clear of matches.
It was pretty clear to him that Delaney Carson was a
blazing torch.

Once again he considered getting out of there. What
did he hope to accomplish? If he'd learned anything in
the last few months it was that sympathy, even well-
meaning, just made things worse. But he couldn't let
her sit there, feeling as though she'd failed. Walking
into that cave after what she'd been through in Baghdad
had taken more sheer guts than he could even imagine.

"I'd say you proved it."

"You're kidding, right?" The laugh she tried failed
miserably. "Unless your definition of success includes
crumpling in a heap, sweating and shaking. Or being
afraid to go to sleep because the flashbacks weave past
and present so tightly it's like suffocating, trying to
break through them again." The look she shot him then
was bitter. "But you wouldn't know about that, would
you, Youngblood? You've never felt weak. I'll bet
you've never failed at anything in your life."

He thought of the shambles his marriage had
become, in large part because he'd been unable to find

a way to make Heather happy. Or maybe, at the end, he'd been unwilling to try. And he thought of Jonny, and his fear that one day he'd have to choose between being close to his son or staying to dutifully care for the grandfather who had taught him what it meant to be born Navajo. "You're wrong," he said softly.

"I don't think I am." He recognized the mercurial change in her mood, as anger chased the self-loathing from her expression. "Why did you come here?" She shoved away from the table, closed the distance between them. "To see if I'd fallen apart completely? Or out of some kind of misguided pity? Because I have to tell you, I've never been much for pity."

"I've never seen a woman less in need of it." She was close, now. Too close. Her eyes weren't clouded by alcohol. They were bright with anger, and other emotions he couldn't identify. Didn't want to identify.

"Or maybe you came here for this, hmm?" Her hands slid up his chest, then did a slow teasing descent. "Did the big, strong, stoic investigator think the little woman was in need of some comforting?" She ran the tip of one index finger along his stomach, where his T-shirt met the waistband of his jeans. Beneath the cloth, his stomach muscles jumped.

He grabbed her hand in his, his grasp tighter than he intended. "Don't."

"Why not? I don't need soothing but I wouldn't mind a distraction. You'd make a hell of a distraction, Youngblood." She went on tiptoe, nipped at the lobe of his ear, before breathing into it, "Joe."

That throaty whisper had his brain fogging, his entire system heating. She lined his jaw with a string of stinging kisses, each one scorching a path straight to his groin. He felt himself harden, and dropped her hand to take her by the waist, push her away. She stepped into his arms as if it were an embrace, her lips brushing his. And the contact had him freezing.

She traced his mouth with the tip of her tongue, before slicking it across his lips. She tasted foreign. Exotic. Forbidden. It hadn't been so long for him that common sense could be overridden by any willing woman. He told himself that even as his fingers curled into her waist, kneading the curves lying beneath thin stretchy fabric.

His lack of participation didn't discourage her. She sampled his mouth with hers, taking his bottom lip between her teeth, not quite gently. She tugged the shirt from the waistband of his jeans, and her cool smooth hands slid up his sides, across his chest, lower.

At his involuntary shudder he felt her lips curve against his, and his discomfort switched abruptly to anger. Maybe she thought she could drive him away by issuing an invitation neither of them had any intention of accepting. Or maybe she really wanted to use him to rid herself of her demons. Either way, he had no intention of obliging. But he would show her the danger of dancing too close to the fire.

Deliberately, he brought her closer, dropping his hands to her hips and pulling her hard against him. She stilled, her eyes widening, and he recognized the wariness that flickered in their depths as he closed the slight distance to her mouth.

He was capable of finesse, but he didn't bother with it. He pressed her lips apart and his tongue swept in, a carnal invasion. It tangled with hers, before sliding along the slick surface of her teeth.

She seemed just a little stunned at his abrupt transition to aggressor, but she didn't pull away. Her lips seemed to soften against his, before parting further in a way that could only be construed as an invitation.

Her hands tightened around his neck and her mouth twisted against his with an unmistakable response that served to fuel his own. A reckless sort of hunger leaped, and reason receded. For a long moment, he allowed himself to set aside responsibility and judgment to indulge in the unexpected riot of sensation.

He turned without releasing her and moved her backward until the wall was at her shoulders. His mouth feasted on hers, drawing out the pleasure to be had from a woman who gave freely, at least this much. Deliberately he pressed her knees apart, stepped between them to press against the inviting notch between her thighs. Dimly it occurred to him that the tiny fleece shorts and skimpy top she wore would be all too easy to dispense with.

Heat flared, sudden and urgent, in the pit of his belly, and he tore his mouth from hers in an effort to salvage his deteriorating control. His lips were distracted by the surprisingly soft skin beneath her ear, and he moved his hand to her nape to hold her still while he investigated the spot that made her shiver against him. Baby soft hair brushed against his knuckles and his fingers delved into the silky waves that she usually scraped up into a knot on the top of her head. Unbidden, an erotic image flashed across his mind of those silky curls brushing against his bare chest. His stomach. Lower.

He had to pull away, to gulp in a needed breath that would summon control once more. But that attempt was shattered as she cupped his face in her smooth palms, ran a light finger across his mouth.

"So serious." A sad little smile curved her lips. "Everything doesn't have to be so serious, does it, Joe?"

The question was its own kind of invitation. If she was offering to keep sex casual between them he could have told her it was too late for that. He hadn't felt *casual* about her since they'd met. Now was the time to walk away. To justify the decision that had brought him here when every instinct had screamed at him that he'd been making a mistake.

But it was getting increasingly difficult to touch her and recall all the reasons this was wrong. She didn't feel wrong. She felt satiny smooth where the curve of her shoulder met the base of her throat; soft where her breasts flattened against his chest; sleek where waist curved to hip; firm in the long length of thigh pressed against his own.

Her fingers slipped beneath his shirt and his blood slowed in his veins, thickened. She pushed up the fabric and leaned to kiss the flesh she'd bared.

Sparks detonated beneath her lips, and he hissed in a breath, his decision, such as it was, made. After

Heather left, it hadn't been difficult to find females willing to help burn off pent-up lust if he'd chosen it. But this was the first he'd *wanted,* with a savage sort of hunger that had alarms shrilling in the back of his mind. That sort of power made this woman dangerous.

He released her to find the hem of her top, drag it upward. She raised her arms so he could tug it over her head in one continuous movement, then shed his T-shirt. That first sensation of flesh against flesh had a low satisfied growl escaping him.

The initial sense of satisfaction was short-lived. He stepped back far enough to cup her breasts, to learn the shape and weight and texture of her. To stroke her velvety nipples, coaxing them into taut sensitive peaks before lowering his head to take one of them in his mouth.

The taste of her was a kick to the system, a sinful flavor that pumped straight to his blood. He gathered her closer and sucked strongly, gratified by her gasp of pleasure.

Her hands streaked over his biceps and shoulders, lingering to test muscle and sinew with clever, teasing fingers. He scraped her nipple lightly with his teeth and it beaded more tightly in his mouth. Her nails bit into his skin in response and something primal inside him exulted at the hint of savagery.

Impatience surged through him. He wanted to touch her everywhere, now, at once. He wanted to find the places that made her shake and sigh, to discover the scent of her in every sweet, secret place. He wanted, more than was comfortable, to take her outside herself, to free her from the past that wove its iron net around her and in the process lose himself in her, just for a little while.

He scraped his thumb over her other nipple, as his tongue tormented its twin. He felt her hands at the waist-band of his jeans, and he shifted his hips away from her frantic fingers. She was becoming a fever in his blood, scorching away any thought of restraint. But he didn't want this to be over. Not yet. There was too much he hadn't touched. Tasted. Experienced. There would be plenty of time when his blood had cooled and reason had returned to consider the ramifications of these moments. There would be time then for regrets. He didn't want one of them to be that it had been over too quickly.

Her breasts were high sweet mounds whose firmness drove him a little crazy. He slid a hand to her thigh, swept down its length and back up again. Felt the whisper of muscle beneath the silky skin and that excited him, too.

She managed to get his jeans unbuttoned so he caught both of her hands in one of his and held them above her head, out of the way. "No," he muttered against her mouth before pausing for another long deep wet kiss. "Wait."

His voice sounded strange to his own ears, hoarse, almost guttural. Nothing about his reaction to her was normal. He didn't recall ever wanting to steep himself in a woman before, to press so close that it was hard to tell where her sensations stopped and where his began.

She twisted in his grasp and panted, "Dammit, Joe."

Primitive satisfaction had him smiling at the frustrated

desire in those two words. "Soon," he promised, sliding his hand down the outside of her leg. He reversed course and she caught her breath as his fingers grazed the sensitive skin inside her shorts, traced the crease where thigh met pelvis. He drew his head back to watch her, and something clenched hard in his chest.

Delaney's eyes were heavy-lidded, the gold expanded around the iris like twin jewels. Her lips were swollen from his, her hair tangled from his fingers and he felt a primordial surge of pleasure at the sight. With one deliberate finger he stroked her, damp heat beneath lace, and she jerked helplessly in response.

There was a roaring in his system, like thunder crashing atop a butte, and watching her pleasure magnified his own. He cupped and stroked her, coaxing her hips to match the rhythm of his movements. Her throat arched and he was driven to test the delicate cord of her neck with his teeth in a primitive taste for flesh.

He slipped his fingers inside the elastic of her panties and covered her mound. His fingertips were moistened with her desire and he slid them over her in a motion meant to torment. Something like a sob escaped her and he increased the pressure, bending to take a nipple in his mouth.

The dual assault had her twisting against him, in a sensual struggle that honed the keen edge of passion, sharp as a blade. And when he stroked one finger inside her dampness, and watched her shatter, the greedy hunger rocketed through him, demanding a release.

He freed her for the moment it took to shed his

clothes and had her back in his arms before her eyes had fluttered all the way open. The look in them was dazed, drugged, and his touch was a shade rough as he pushed her shorts over the curve of her hips, down the silky length of thigh and kicked them away.

He cupped her bottom and lifted her, stepping between her open thighs and barely managed to restrain himself from entering her with one urgent thrust. The passion was pounding in his veins, careening through his blood until his every sense was focused on the burning need to bury himself in her. He pressed her back against the wall, and positioned her legs, growling when she locked her ankles around his hips.

Her fingers found him then, in one lingering firm stroke that had his vision hazing and his senses fogging. He pressed against her sweet yielding flesh and buried himself to the hilt. There was a stunning moment of clarity where he was aware of every individual heightened sensation. The trickle of perspiration on his back, the blood hammering in his veins, the bite of Delaney's nails on his shoulders, the sweet clutch and release of her inner muscles working against his hardness.

And then clarity exploded in a wash of savage hunger and he surged against her, control lost, over and over, trying to get closer. Deeper. His vision narrowed until she was the only point in it as flesh slapped against flesh and she strained and shuddered against him.

He heard her cry out and he pounded into her faster,

frantic now. Then pleasure abruptly slammed into him, spun him up and over the edge into a vortex of sensation.

Fingers of sunlight were slanting through the blinds and across Delaney's face, creating enough heat that she awakened, uncomfortably warm. She opened one eye to glare balefully at the offending blind, before dragging open the other eyelid. As always upon awakening, her brain was sluggish. The first thing she was going to buy, she vowed, was some room-darkening shades. She sat up, kicked at the sheet twisted around her ankles and yawned. Maybe even a small window air conditioner. One that would keep her cool enough that she wouldn't haven't to sleep nude.

Nude. Her gaze bounced down, widened. Leaning over she yanked at the sheet and pulled it up, her mind in shock. She shouldn't be nude. She'd had shorts on. A shirt. She distinctly remembered…

She fell back on the bed with a mortified groan. She distinctly remembered all but inviting Joe Youngblood to tear her clothes off of her. And if memory served, it hadn't taken all that much coaxing for him to do just that. She yanked a pillow over her face to shut out the humiliating recollection. But it wouldn't be so easily banished. The problem with orgasms was that they only wiped the mind clean for a few moments. Well, substantially longer if people knew what they were doing and could, somehow, string round one with rounds two and three so smoothly that it felt like one long, mind-shattering free fall into pleasure.

Joe Youngblood had definitely known what he was doing.

Do I need a condom?

She shivered at the recollection of his voice. It had been a little late to ask since he'd carried her from the kitchen to the bed and had already been buried deep inside her again. But at least he'd summoned the brainpower to think of protection eventually. She hadn't even given it a moment's consideration, which made her ever-grateful for the contraceptive patch on her hip. Apparently she'd undergone more changes than she'd thought in the last couple years if she could so easily forget basic sexual safety.

The pillow was tossed aside, and she stared at the ceiling broodingly. One of the only positives for having made her share of mistakes is that it gave her a point of reference. Sleeping with Joe Youngblood wasn't the worst error she'd ever made in her life. But God help her, it ranked right up there. She'd spent the night having mind-blowing sex with a man she barely knew and who was going to be darn hard to avoid in the future.

But she hadn't dreamed.

She hadn't struggled beneath an oppressive blanket of PTSD nightmares that could suck her into their vortex and leave her feeling weak and frightened and hopeless. She supposed she had Joe Youngblood to thank for that, but somehow she couldn't summon a speck of gratitude.

Chapter 5

The shadow-shrouded alley smelled like death. Joe peered through the gloom, gun drawn, and hoped the odor wasn't an omen. He nudged Arnie and jerked his head toward the overflowing Dumpster against the wall of the next building. Arnie nodded, and they fanned out, approaching carefully. Quintero had been wilier than they'd given him credit for. They'd arrived at his apartment shortly after dawn, warrant in hand. But the drug dealer had gone out the bedroom window as they'd been coming through the front door. He'd disappeared into the alley moments before and the large refuse container offered the best chance of concealment.

Joe held up one hand, and his partner halted, gun trained on the Dumpster. Joe went on silently, spinning rapidly around the other side. The space was empty.

He glanced back at Arnie, the two men communicating silently. While his partner stayed put, Joe checked the rest of the dingy area.

Nothing. Joe turned around, headed back toward Arnie. He was still three yards away when he saw the first sign of movement from the pile of debris inside the Dumpster.

"Down, get down!" He leaped to the side as he shouted, a split second before the area exploded in gunfire. The scene fragmented into stills. Quintero rising from the garbage, his automatic spraying bullets. Arnie stumbling backward, falling against the building. Sliding down its wall to the rubbish-strewn ground.

Joe dived toward his friend, his sights on Quintero as the man turned the gun on him. They fired at the same time, and Joe hit the ground, shielding Arnie's prone body, prepared to shoot again.

But Quintero was slumped over the front of the Dumpster, his body motionless. As Joe watched, the man's gun slipped from his hand, clattered to the ground.

"He dead?" Arnie mumbled.

The sound of his partner's voice had never sounded so good. "Are you?" Joe shot him a quick look, noting the blood running freely down his arm, before turning a watchful gaze back on the dealer.

"Not...even...close." Arnie stifled a moan as he shifted position, cursed colorfully in English before switching to Spanish. Navajo was too precise a language to lend itself to eloquent cursing. The halting string of obscenities eased Joe's worry.

Keeping his gun trained on Quintero, Joe pulled his radio from his belt and called for an ambulance. Then he approached the dealer.

He reached out to grab the man's hair, lifted his head. Quintero's eyes fluttered, then slid closed again. "You made some bad mistakes all around. You can fix one, though. Give us your supplier's name. That's all we want. We'll have help here in a few minutes."

But when Joe heard the breath whistling through the man's chest, he knew that the ambulance wasn't going to be there in time. Quintero's lips were moving, but Joe had to lean close to make out the words.

"Go…to…hell."

The distant sound of sirens could already be heard, but the man's body had gone limp. Joe released him and eased away. Hell was an Anglo concept, not a Navajo one. But if it did exist, he was pretty sure Quintero was already on his way there.

Arnie had already been taken away to the hospital, but Joe waited for FBI agent Delmer Mitchell to arrive on the scene. Another member of the task force, he was investigating the suspected drug-related homicides of three Navajo youth two weeks earlier.

Joe stood a ways off as the agent went through Quintero's pockets. "Seems like your job would be easier if you could just do this yourself."

Joe didn't bother answering. The Navajo aversion to

death was too deeply ingrained in him to be put aside simply to conduct the search, and he knew it was useless to try and explain it to the *belagana*. Mitchell held up a cell phone, car keys and a large wad of cash. "This is it." He got to his feet, holding the contents up for Joe's perusal.

Shoving aside his distaste at touching the dead man's belongings, he took the cell phone and turned it over, studying it. It looked like one of the disposables that were showing up in nearby department stores. Many of the homes on Navajo Nation lands still didn't have landlines but cell phones were getting increasingly common, though the coverage was sporadic. Some criminals assumed they were untraceable with the use of prepaid plans. Joe was hoping that didn't turn out to be the case.

He pressed the button to list the incoming call log and was unsurprised to find it empty. The same was true of the outgoing log. But when he hit Redial a number appeared on the screen and a hard smile crossed his lips.

A whistle escaped Mitchell's lips. "The guy was carrying over five thousand dollars." He looked at Joe. "You get anything?"

"Maybe." He didn't have much time. He'd have to follow up on the caller before news of Quintero's death got out. "I'm going to search his apartment. And then I'll find out whether or not this number leads anywhere."

"Good-sized bust?" Captain Tapahe leaned back in his chair, working his shoulders tiredly.

Standing before the man's desk, Joe nodded. "About three kilos of ice. Street value would be about a million, a million point three."

Tapahe's face brightened. "Not bad. Maybe he's our guy after all."

Joe shook his head. "I don't think so. I was surprised Quintero has risen that high in the feeding chain, but he doesn't have the brains to coordinate the kind of network we're tracking. He was strictly a middleman, and he wasn't interested in sharing the name of his supplier."

"Well, he won't be talking now," The captain's voice was matter-of-fact. "The warrant turn up anything in his apartment?"

Joe shifted his weight. His left knee had taken the brunt of his fall that afternoon, and it was throbbing. "He had a throwaway cell phone on him. There were no calls logged on the incoming or outgoing list, but I was able to retrieve one number by hitting Redial." The captain looked hopeful. "I sent a text message pretending to be Quintero, arranging to meet the guy in back of McDonald's. Ran the number on the Avalanche he was driving. Showed up registered to Brant Graywolf." Joe was familiar with the prominent family name and the kid's juvie sheet.

"Not surprising," the captain grunted. "The kid's been in and out of drugs for years. Quintero was probably his supplier. Did you question him?"

"I plan to round up all of Quintero's known clients and acquaintances. Brant goes to the top of the list. I'm hoping Lucas Tallhorse can perform a dump on the cell and retrieve the incoming and outgoing call logs." It went without saying that the NTP lacked the funds for specialized technicians. But Officer Tallhorse had proven to be a pretty decent techie in his own right. If Tapahe okayed it, the chief would let the man give the phone a shot, in lieu of his other duties.

The captain nodded. "I'll make sure he gets to it. Did you find anything else of interest during the search?"

"He was carrying over five thousand on him, and we found another twenty grand in a shoe box stashed under some floorboards beneath the bed." The man's imagination hadn't exceeded his IQ.

"I've got something else here for you." The captain riffled through the piles of papers on his desk until he came up with a scribbled note, which he handed to Joe. "A Hank Yazzie was busted last night for selling liquor out of his garage. Guess he had quite a business going. Anyway, he's trying to cut a deal and offered up some information about the homicides Mitchell's investigating."

Joe felt interest stirring. "Anything that sounded credible?"

Tapahe shrugged. "It might be bogus, but he mentioned Quintero. Said he sold alcohol to Oree and that they sometimes drank together. One of those times, just last week he claims, Quintero mentioned something about the murders. Yazzie thinks he may have been involved."

Joe narrowed his gaze, considering. With the recent government crackdown on the ingredients for the cheaper, easier-to-make meth, more and more addicts were turning to the crystal ice Quintero had been selling. Because ice was substantially more expensive, there was a corresponding rise in burglaries and robberies as addicts sought to support their habit. But the increased crime rate they'd been experiencing hadn't prepared any of them for the sheer brutality of the execution-style murder of the three young men. Homicides were still relatively infrequent on the reservation. If Quintero had been involved in that, he'd been more dangerous than Joe had realized.

Joe tucked the note in his pocket. "I'll pass this on to Agent Mitchell. He might want to talk to Yazzie himself." He'd let the fed determine if there was any truth in the man's talk. "What have you heard about Arnie's condition?"

A smile cracked Tapahe's countenance for the first time. "He's going to be okay. Bucking for discharge, and barring that, offering bribes to anyone who'll bring him a cheeseburger."

Relief eased the knot in Joe's chest. Arnie had assured him he was all right, but Joe hadn't been able to get any such reassurance from the medics who'd arrived on the scene. And the aftermath of the shooting and search had kept him occupied for hours.

The captain continued. "They dug one bullet out of his arm. The Kevlar stopped the other one. Lucky thing. Would have hit him in the heart. That's why they're keeping him. They want to monitor his heart for bruising."

Joe winced in sympathy. The vests were lifesavers but they didn't deflect a bullet, just caught and spread its momentum over a larger portion of the body. Arnie was lucky the vest had prevented the bullet from penetrating the skin.

Glancing at his watch, Joe said, "I'll swing by the hospital on the way home."

"You do that. But don't let him talk you into smuggling him some fries."

Joe walked out without making any promises. It was hard to tell when he might be in Arnie's position, and it never hurt to rack up a few points to call in whenever that time might come.

"The mutton stew was excellent." Delaney leaned back in her chair and smiled across the table at Charley Youngblood. "And fry bread has just gone on my list of favorites."

"It was my pleasure." The older man spoke with a courtliness that was as much a part of him as his seamed weathered face. He was dressed in what seemed a uniform of sorts on the Navajo lands: jeans, Western-style shirt and cowboy boots. Hammered silver and turquoise wristbands encircled his wrists, and his long gray hair was gathered into a tight roll at the nape of his neck and bound with yarn. "I don't often have guests. Next time you stay for dinner you must try *nitsid digoohi,* kneel-down corn bread. I think you'll like that, as well."

"I'm looking forward to sampling many of the

traditional foods during the course of my work here."
And if this afternoon was any indication, she was going
to enjoy writing this book even more than she'd
expected. Charley Youngblood was clearly a tradition-
alist, and a fascinating source of Navajo lore. They'd
spent hours talking about native legends, and she'd
found him a natural storyteller, with a gift for creating
intriguing windows into his culture's past. Already she
was toying with the idea of organizing the book to
allow entire quotes, complete with photos, of people
like Charley who contributed to it. She doubted she
could replicate the sheer magic of his words.

The time spent in his company had been soothing.
It was easy to immerse herself in the project as she
listened to him retell the Creation story, the tale of
Changing Woman, the Sun the Moon and the Stars.
Easy to forget, at least for a time, his relationship to the
man she couldn't quite push from her thoughts.

She could feel her cheeks heat at the memory of last
night. She'd felt awkward coming here today, given what
had transpired between her and Joe, even realizing
Charley wouldn't be aware of it. The only thing that had
eased her discomfort was knowing Joe would be at work.
She didn't want a chance encounter with him here.

She didn't want a chance encounter with him
anywhere. But she wasn't naive enough to think she
could avoid him indefinitely. Given enough time, she
would, however, be ready to face him again with
defenses firmly realigned.

Her gaze traveled over the interior of the house. The

log structure was six-sided, she assumed to emulate some of the traditional hogans. The interior was comprised of one large living space. The main area was simply yet comfortably furnished with an overstuffed couch and armchairs. The dining area was tucked into one corner, partitioned from the galley kitchen by a counter. A hallway leading to the back of the home led to what she assumed would be bedrooms and a bath.

She'd heard that some on Navajo Nation lands lived without electricity and running water, but Charley's home was equipped with both. He had a phone but no television or any of the other electronic gadgetry that many took for granted.

The older man rose and began to clear the table, waving her away when she rose and stacked the remaining dishes.

Charley turned to take the dishes from her, and once again shooed her away. "You are my guest," he said firmly.

Her mother's strictures about politeness didn't always apply when she was immersed in foreign cultures. Delaney had learned over the years it was far more civil to follow her host's wishes than to tussle over sharing the chores, despite the manners Sabrina Carson had drilled into her three children.

Wandering into the main area, Delaney studied the rugs and wall hangings, presumably done by local weavers. Beneath one was an eight-by-ten picture of Charley with a young boy that she'd noticed earlier.

"My great-grandson, Jonny," Charley said, coming into the room and noting her interest. His voice was filled with pride, and something else, something she couldn't quite identify. "He looks much like Joseph at that age, although I don't remember my grandson getting into quite as much mischief."

Shock whipped through her. Joe Youngblood was a *father?* Maybe even *married?*

Speechless, Delaney stared at the picture again. But try as she might, she couldn't imagine Joe as a doting father. Laughing with his small son. Playing games. Tucking him into bed.

The mental image widened to include a nameless, faceless woman. A wife. She hauled in a breath, feeling a little nauseated. She'd assumed Joe was single, because he hadn't said otherwise. But she knew some men wouldn't refrain from taking any willing woman that came across their path, married or not.

And she'd all but hurtled herself into his arms.

Wincing inwardly, she managed, "He has your eyes."

"Many have said so." It was impossible to miss the satisfaction in Charley's voice as he came to her side and picked up the picture. "When he's in the room, he fills it with light. Small boys are all energy, you know."

What Delaney knew about children wouldn't fill a teacup. She had more pressing concerns at the moment. "I didn't realize your grandson was married."

"I'm not."

She froze at the sound of that familiar voice, for just an instant. Then she turned, tucking the tips of her fingers in the back pockets of her jeans, and surveyed the man she'd sworn she wouldn't react to again.

"Maybe you should wear a little bell around your neck. That way your silent entrances won't endanger people with cardiac arrest."

Joe shut the door behind him, his gaze traveling to the man standing beside her. "Grandfather."

"Joseph." Charley replaced the picture while Delaney watched the two of them closely. Their polite tones belied the palpable undercurrents eddying between them. "I heard about Arnie. Is he all right?"

"I just saw him. He's already bullying the nurses about his release. He could be back on the job in a few days." Joe walked into the center of the room and immediately shrank it with his presence. The realization had Delaney's earlier vow evaporating. A woman would have to be dead not to respond to this man.

With both Youngblood men in the same room it occurred to her again how little they resembled each other. Joe was close to six foot, with finer, sharper features than the older man. His nose was narrow and straight, the thick dark hair she'd had her fingers twisted in last night was worn short. And while Charley emanated a quiet dignity that immediately commanded respect, Joe radiated a subtle menace that induced wariness. As well as a raw sexuality that gripped a woman by the throat and ripped a reaction from her.

Steeling herself, she schooled her expression to polite interest. "Your grandfather is a wonderful host. He spent the afternoon explaining some of the better-known Navajo legends and then followed up his hospitality with a delicious meal."

"You've been here all day?"

She wondered how a voice could be expressionless and still hold a note of censure. He must work at it.

Charley saved her from answering. "I was just going to offer to show Delaney the hogan and the sweat house."

The idea was appealing but making a sudden decision, she moved toward Charley, not caring in the slightest that she was turning her back on Joe. "You know, it's just occurred to me how much of your time I've taken up today. I get like that when I'm engrossed in something, I'm afraid." She reached over to squeeze his hand. "Thank you for your hospitality, but I'm going to give you time to visit with...your grandson. We can continue this whenever it's convenient for you."

They decided on a time the next day and she collected her equipment, all the while aware of Joe's inscrutable gaze on her. "Until tomorrow, then."

"I'll help you get this to your Jeep."

Joe slung the strap of her camera case over his shoulder and picked up her tripod. Delaney clenched her jaw at his high-handedness. "That's okay. I can get it."

"It's no problem." Leaving her with the bag containing her tape recorder and notebooks, he strode to the door. Because she had no choice, she told Charley goodbye and followed.

Joe had already stowed the equipment in the backseat and started the ignition before Delaney caught up with him. She put her bag in the backseat next to the camera and slammed the door with more force than necessary. "In a hurry to get me out of here?"

"Your Jeep has been sitting in the sun all day. It's going to take a while for the air conditioner to cool it." His hand clamped on her arm when she would have opened the driver's door.

A current of electricity seemed to transfer from his hand to her arm. Ignoring it, she looked pointedly at his hand, then at him. "Was there something else?"

"Yeah. I want you to be careful not to wear Charley out. He won't say anything, but he tires easily."

She cocked a brow. "Sure wish I'd known that before I had him running laps around the edge of the property today."

At her sardonic tone, Joe's words grew clipped. "He had triple bypass surgery three months ago. He's still recovering. Keep that in mind."

Concern filled her. "He didn't mention it."

"He wouldn't. So I am."

Silence stretched, their gazes locked. There was no sign of the lover from last night who had pounded himself into her with a fierce need that had matched her own. She swallowed, the memory turning her knees weak. Deliberately stiffening them, she said, "We weren't discussing you, you know. When you came in. I was just surprised when your grandfather said the boy was yours. At first I thought…I was afraid…"

"You thought I'd screwed around on my wife with you."

Though she knew his words were deliberately chosen to maximize her discomfort, she didn't look away. "I don't cheat," she said simply. "And I don't sleep with men who do. But I didn't ask you before, and I'm finding it a little hard to forgive myself for not making sure first."

Although his expression didn't alter, something in it seemed to ease infinitesimally. "I'm divorced, but not because I ever cheated on my wife."

She drew in a breath, then barreled on. "Last night was…" A colossal error in judgment. Amazing. Fantastic. Fraught with complications. "Well, it shouldn't have happened." It was difficult to think while pinned by that unwavering stare. She strove for a flippant tone, thought she managed it well enough. "If you're worrying that I'm going to try to throw all sorts of strings on you, don't be. It was a onetime thing. You had the good fortune to be seduced by a desperate woman but not one who's interested in a repeat."

"Don't kid yourself." There was a light in his eyes, a dangerous burn. His grip on her arm had loosened, but his thumb skated over the veins in her wrist, making the skin there tingle. "You didn't take me anywhere I didn't want to go. Did it feel like you were alone in that bed? Or against that wall? I was inside you because that's what I wanted. Not because you gave me permission or because I asked for it. And when I want that again—when we both do—I won't need to ask permission then, either."

He released her and she leaned bonelessly against the Jeep, barely feeling the hot metal beneath the material of her thin T-shirt. Her voice, when she found it, sounded irritatingly breathless. "I think it's best if we keep our interactions to a minimum in the future."

"Do you?" His smile was humorless. "Then you're not going to be too happy when I tell you I plan to come over as soon as I speak to my grandfather."

Anger blessedly cut through her stupor. "Maybe I wasn't clear enough earlier."

"I think we understand each other." While she searched those words for hidden meaning, he went on. "You downloaded those pictures today, right? The ones you took yesterday? I told you I want to see them. I'll be over in a couple hours."

No. That was out of the question. "I'll make copies and drop them off at police headquarters tomorrow."

"I want to see them tonight. I'll be by later."

When she finally found her voice again he was already walking away. "No, don't do that. Joe. Joe!" She was still calling impotently after him when he walked into his grandfather's cabin and shut the door behind him.

"A delightful woman," Charley said as Joe closed the door on Delaney's voice. "But older than her years, I think."

Joe shrugged. The last thing he wanted to discuss with his grandfather was Delaney Carson. He'd been unable to banish her from his thoughts all day. "How'd you hear about Arnie?" He crossed the room to an easy chair, waited respectfully until his grandfather had poured them both coffee, handed Joe a mug and seated himself. Only then did Joe sit.

"Lucy Bai called me. She and Arnie are *Ashiihi*. She

knew you two worked together and wanted to know if you had been hurt, too."

Joe nodded. In the Anglo way, the fact that Arnie and Lucy were of the Salt Clan would make them cousins, but Navajos consider members of the same clan as brother and sister. "I'm sorry if hearing the news that way worried you. I'm fine."

"I long ago came to terms with the danger of your job, Joseph. But I also can't help but worry. So," he brought the coffee to his lips, sipped, "Did you catch this man? Lock him up in your jail?"

Joe hesitated. His idea of justice rarely reconciled with that of his grandfather. Charley believed that all bad behavior was caused by the criminals' disharmony. Rather than prison, the only way to help them was with a Mountain Way ceremony, to drive the dark wind out of them and restore them to *hozho*, with all their friends and relatives gathered to support them

"No. There were shots fired. Arnie was hit. The drug dealer who shot him was killed."

Distress flickered over Charley's face. But he said only, "You must be watchful, Joseph." Although it was customary to avoid speaking of it, Joe knew his grandfather referred to the *chindi*—or ghost that each person releases when they die—an evil force that returns to avenge offenses.

"I will be." At times it felt like a balancing act to straddle two worlds. And yet he could no more reject one than he could the other. So he lived in the American culture that permeated every part of the country while remaining connected to the teachings of his *Diné* roots. The resulting mixture wasn't always one his grandfather understood, but it brought harmony to Joe.

"You're looking well. You must have succeeded in cleaning out your friends on Monday night."

Charley chuckled. "I did all right, although not as well as Larry Blackwater. That was fine with me. Now he's the one the others don't want back."

"I came by to see you that night. I forgot you'd be out." Joe hooked a booted ankle on his knee. "I know we disagree on this photo history project, but I meant no disrespect."

"We both have strong opinions." Charley shrugged, as if it were of no consequence. "You're too much like me. And maybe like your mother, as well. She has trouble hearing ideas that aren't her own."

Joe stiffened at the mention of his mother, at the trace of wistful indulgence in his grandfather's voice. Charley would never stop missing the daughter who derided the very way of life he cherished. Joe had been no more than Jonny's age when he realized that her infrequent visits to the reservation were always driven more by a need for money than sentiment. Navajo culture was matriarchal in nature, but Joe had little use for the woman who had borne him at seventeen, only to disappear months later. As far as he was concerned, the best thing she'd ever done for him was to allow her father to raise him.

"And what do you think of our Delaney Carson now?"

The non sequitur had Joe freezing, his mind flashing back to an image of Delaney pressed between the wall of the kitchen and his body. He could almost feel the heat of her again, taste her flavor. Just that mental lapse was enough to have his blood thickening, his gut clenching.

"What about her?" He brought the mug to his lips, took his time drinking.

"She told me that the two of you had met. Given her résumé, I had expected someone older. But there's something about her. I think she'll win over many of those who opposed her hiring. And others may become convinced when they see what her name means to this book project."

Joe stilled. "What about her name?"

"She won a Pulitzer Prize for international reporting. I understand that she went back to Iraq after her injuries were treated to continue her work." Charley paused to drink slowly, savoring the brew. Caffeine was one of the things in his diet that his heart doctor strictly rationed. "This will be the first project she's undertaken since, so it will receive a great deal of publicity simply because it has her name attached to it. This book could bring a great deal of publicity to the tribe."

Joe's fingers clenched tightly on the mug. He was recalling the sight of Delaney's face after she'd burst from the cave. As she sat, head bowed, staring miserably at the bottle of Absolut on the kitchen table. Something ignited in his chest at the thought of the tribe trading on the very experiences that had scarred her, that still caused her such pain.

He leaned forward, set the mug on the table in front

of him, and wondered uneasily where this unfamiliar surge of protectiveness had come from. He barely knew the woman. One night of sex, no matter how hot, didn't change that. But he knew enough about her to be certain she wouldn't thank him for his concern.

Last night was a onetime thing.

Her earlier words shouldn't have summoned an instant primordial possessiveness, one he'd barely recognized. She was right, and he realized that. Getting involved with any woman right now was a distraction he could ill afford.

But getting involved with one who could make him feel…that was a disaster waiting to happen. And a risk he wasn't willing to take.

Chapter 6

"Obviously you weren't told 'no' often enough as a child. You have a problem with the word." Delaney's tone was caustic, lest he think that opening the door for him was a welcoming gesture. There was no use trying to keep him out. He'd already proved, on numerous occasions, that he didn't regard a shut or locked door as any particular deterrent.

"You have the photos. You have the equipment to work with them and print them." He walked into the house and faced her. "I've got a case that's taking up all my time at work. It doesn't make sense to add on one more task tomorrow when I can just as easily see them here, tonight."

His logical tone was nearly as annoying as his

presence. But when he walked through the house toward the spare bedroom where he'd surprised her that first night, she let the screen door bang shut and hurried after him. "Don't touch anything."

He hitched a hip on the corner of her desk. "Let's see what you've got."

She picked up a stack of photos and a magnifying glass, and handed them to him. "I'm just taking a closer look at them now." At his sharp glance, she snapped, "I've been busy. I do have a job to do here, you know."

Joe flipped through the pictures quickly, then started through them again, this time with the magnifying glass, to study them more closely. "You took this many shots of one place?"

Delaney rolled her eyes and sat down at the computer, trying to ignore the fact that his stance placed him in disturbingly close proximity. Quickly, she selected the appropriate photo folder on the screen and opened it. "It's not uncommon for me to take twice as many shots to get one or two I can use. That's one of the advantages of digital. There's so much less waste. I can delete the ones of poorer quality without ever printing them."

The first of the photos filled the screen. With swift movements she set up enlarging the photo in ten percent increments. He looked up and scanned the room. "You have more equipment in here than before."

"It arrived this morning." And she'd fussed over it like a mother hen until it had been time to set off for Charley's. She gave little thought to clothes or jewelry, but when it came to her photography and computer equipment, she spared no expense. "I numbered the pictures on the back, and they're in the order I took them. I was using a zoom at first, before switching to a wide angle when I got closer."

Joe peered more closely through the magnifying glass at the picture in his hand. "And you thought the shots were fired from the top of the cliff?"

"They seemed to be." She brought up another picture, enlarged it and then began zooming in on sections along the top of the cliff. "But after the first couple I wasn't really paying attention. I was too busy trying to survive."

He looked at the screen and lowered the magnifying glass. "What's that?" He tapped an area on the computer screen with an index finger.

"Reflection, probably."

"Yeah, but off what?" He slid from his perch and knelt next to her.

She zoomed in on the section once, then again. Other than the spot of light he'd noted, there was nothing to see. Disappointed, she sat back in the chair. "The angle probably caught a streak of mineral in the rock. The photos before and right after this one don't show anything." She continued clicking on the individual photos, zooming in on sections along the top of the cliff line. It was a tedious process, made more so by her heightened awareness of the man inches away from her.

He was too close. Hadn't she told herself that they should never get this near again? Hadn't she told *him?*

Apparently her hormones didn't heed advice because they were humming to life. Which only went to prove they operated separate from good sense.

Grimly, she inched a little over in her seat, to place a bit more distance between them as she cropped a photo on the screen and enlarged it. Despite his reaction earlier when she'd set the new boundaries between them, Joe didn't appear to be experiencing any problems by working this closely with her. She stole a glance at him, but he was once again absorbed in the stack of photos. It was a kick to the ego to see how little effect she had on him, especially since his nearness was playing havoc with her concentration.

Reid had had the same sort of focus, she recalled with a pang. Despite what went on between them personally, he had always been able to switch his attention from her to the job with an ease that had stung more than a little. Not that she needed, or wanted, a man's undivided attention at all times. But she'd come to accept that she was never going to be as important to Reid as the story, whatever it happened to be.

It had been the love of the job that had brought them together. In her darkest moments she wondered if the story was the only real bond they shared. He'd loved her, as much as he was capable. She'd always wonder if that would've been enough. If it would have ever stopped feeling like little slices to the heart every time he'd shut her out, shut himself away.

She'd never had the opportunity to find out. He'd

died with seventy-one others in that hotel blast and her life had never been the same.

The memory had her defenses slamming firmly in place. She'd never go through that again. It was easier, far easier, to be the one who backed away. Maybe she'd wounded Joe's pride by being the first to point out what a mistake last night was, but she couldn't believe he wouldn't have arrived at the same conclusion on his own.

He hadn't exactly struck her as a man looking for a serious relationship, at any point.

Immersed in her own thoughts, she almost missed it. She'd moved on to another part of the photo she was examining when her mind caught up with her subconscious. Quickly she went back to the section she'd just zoomed in on. Patiently, Delaney readjusted the picture until she had a clear view of the portion that had caught her attention.

"What does this look like to you?"

Immediately Joe leaned over to study the screen. A hard satisfied smile crossed his lips. "A person's forehead."

"Exactly." Pursing her lips, Delaney hit the command keys to print out a copy of the enlarged photo. "Like he was crouched behind that outcrop of rock up there, with only a portion of his head visible."

"Let's see what else you can get. It'll be tough to identify him by his hairline."

Delaney made a face at him but he'd already turned to leave the room. He was back a moment later with one of her kitchen chairs. "Move over."

Although she wasn't pleased at being ordered around in her own home, she did as he directed to avoid having him in her lap. "I didn't notice that, even with the magnifying glass," Joe murmured, snatching up the photo as soon as the printer finished it.

Eagerly, she brought up the next photo, taking painstaking care to enlarge the spot where the forehead had appeared in the previous picture. Nothing could be seen. Clamping down a quick surge of disappointment, she searched the rest of the photo just as carefully before bringing up the next one. She checked the clock in the corner of her computer screen. "This is going to take a while," she pointed out. She could feel the heat emanating from Joe's body. And it was all too easy to recall that same warmth when his bare flesh pressed against hers.

Nerve endings prickled at the memory, and her skin seemed to shrink two sizes. She needed time and distance to regain her equilibrium. It wasn't so much to ask, was it? The last thirty-six hours had been enough to knock anyone off their stride. It didn't mean she was weak to want a little space. It was only logical, and she would welcome a little logic in her life right about now.

"You should just let me finish this alone. It could be hours," she stressed, as he looked at her with that fathomless gaze. "Whatever I discover, I could make copies and drop them by work. Tomorrow. You could see them first thing."

"But if I stay I can see them now," he pointed out reasonably. "I have a lot going on at work. I doubt you'd catch me in. And Taos made it clear that you're a priority and that he wants me to personally check into this matter."

For a moment she forgot her eagerness to have him gone and stared at him, dismay filling her. It hadn't really occurred to her what it would mean to have her shooting incident dumped on top of Joe's probably already formidable caseload. "When do you plan on sleeping?" she asked bluntly.

Something like humor crossed his expression, although he didn't smile. "Sleep is overrated."

Especially when beds could be used for so much more interesting things.

Shoving that thought aside, Delancy turned back to the computer. She could do this. She would. A few more hours, tops, and she'd be rid of Joe Youngblood and these pesky hormone-driven mental lapses. Then she'd concentrate on the job she'd accepted, the project that had brought her here. He wasn't the only one with work to focus on.

She slapped at his hands when he tried to make adjustments to the picture on the screen. "Do you mind?" With a few quick commands she zoomed in on a section, and then just as quickly discarded it as useless.

"You're touchy tonight." His voice was too bland not to be deliberate. "Any particular reason for that?"

Forcing herself to meet his gaze, she lied through her teeth. "I guess I'm just as possessive of my computer as you are of your gun."

"And if I promise to stay away from the bullet key?"

She refused to let herself smile. "Two jokes in two

days, Youngblood. Careful. Someone might think you have a sense of humor."

They worked in silence for a time, and after a while she almost forgot to be distracted by his nearness. She'd gone through at least five more photos before they both stared at a section of a photo and said simultaneously, "There."

Delaney adjusted the portion and leaned in, trying to see around Joe as he examined their finding. It was the upper right quadrant of a man's face. Part of a forehead, one eye, cheek and the shadow of a nose. "Could be Indian. Maybe Mexican," Joe muttered. "Can you get any closer?"

"Not without distorting it." She showed him what happened when she tried to enlarge it further, then returned to the former shot.

He shook his head, frustration sounding in his voice. "It's still not enough to identify him."

"Not yet." She used her toolbar to trace the man's visible features, and then selected another program to provide them with a blank drawing grid. Pasting the features on the page, she returned to the photos with renewed eagerness and began searching and zooming again. "We may not be lucky enough to get a full-face shot. But maybe we'll get enough to piece together a reasonable resemblance. Enough anyway to ID him."

Hours went by, but filled with a renewed sense of purpose Delaney didn't really notice. After going through the entire assortment of photos, they had four more that provided them with pieces to add to the grid. As well as two chilling partial shots of a rifle muzzle aimed in what must have been her direction.

Joe watched in silence while she manipulated the bits of the shooter's face on the grid, like clicking puzzle pieces together, until she had a fair representation of a person, minus the lower left quadrant of his features.

"That's not bad," he said, studying it. "You even managed to get the parts close in size, proportionately. I think our composite artist will be able to sketch in the rest."

"And then what?" She yawned, and worked her shoulders to dislodge the stiffness there.

"I'll compare it to shots in the mug file, see if I can find a match. Show it to whoever owns that property."

He stood, forcing her to push her chair back and rise, as well. "And then what?"

"Then I'll have to take a trip back there and start talking to families in the area."

She yawned again and began to follow him out of the room. It wasn't until she reached the doorway and nearly bumped into him that she realized he'd stopped to lean against the doorjamb, eyes on her.

Delaney had a crazy flashback to the first time she'd seen him, in almost the same spot, almost the exact position. She'd been afraid to squeeze by him that time, too, but for a very different reason. This time she knew precisely how his hard frame would feel pressed against hers and it was that knowledge that kept her rooted in place.

He was silent for long moments, his gaze brooding. Her patience whittled away by lack of sleep, she finally snapped, "What?"

"I've been thinking about what you said this afternoon. About not repeating what happened between us last night."

There was a buzzing in her ears, a warmth creeping down her spine. "I think that would be best."

"Probably. Smartest, too. Are we going to be smart, Delaney?" His black gaze bore into hers and the space between them seemed to shrink.

No, shrieked a voice deep inside her, one that had gotten her in trouble in the past. *No, no, no!*

"Yes," she said firmly, and clutched her arms to keep her hands from trembling. "We are."

There was a ghost of a smile on his lips, so fleeting that she blinked, wondering if it had been there at all.

He didn't agree or disagree, for which she was grateful, just gave her one last long look and said, "Lock the door after me." Then he walked away.

She followed him to the door, this time at a safe distance, noting that it was past three. He couldn't have left much before five yesterday morning. He had to be exhausted. It was on the tip of her tongue to tell him to be careful, but she swallowed the words.

She'd be wise to heed her own warning. Because if the last couple days had proved anything at all, she was the one who needed to be careful where Joe Young-blood was concerned.

* * *

"I already told you. That wasn't my phone. I found it at a party and picked it up, thinking it belonged to a buddy of mine. So what?" Brant Graywolf stared at Joe across the table of the interview room the next morning and gave a bored hitch of his shoulder. "When you messaged me I figured I'd pull a prank on one of his friends and show up instead of him."

"And did it belong to one of your friends?"

"Guess not. I threw it away after I found that out. I don't even know this Quintero guy you're talking about."

"That's what you keep saying." Joe didn't bother to mask his derision. "But you know what I think? I think you were one of his clients. How about it, Brant? You score from Quintero? Was he your supplier?"

The boy never lost his poise. "I already told you. I don't do drugs anymore. I'm done with all that."

That earnest schoolboy look might have fooled his teachers and coaches when he was a star athlete at Tuba City High. Might have scammed his father into believing that the boy on whom he'd showered every conceivable material possession was finally done sowing his wild oats.

But it didn't convince Joe. His BS detector was better developed than most. If an adult had done half of what Graywolf had done as a juvenile, he'd have been in prison.

Joe crossed his arms and gave the boy a mocking smile. "So getting kicked out of three colleges for possession scared you straight, huh? Wish I could believe that."

"Believe it. *Sir*." The earnest facade cracked a little, allowing some of his cockiness through. "I'm going back to school in the fall and turning over a new leaf. Just ask my dad."

The mention of the boy's father was probably meant to intimidate. The Graywolf family owned and operated the largest construction firm in the area, with a half-dozen branch offices scattered throughout the Southwest. But neither the family's wealth nor stature in the community meant jack to Joe. Somehow this kid was connected to Quintero. Joe was willing to bet that Oree's phone would prove it, too.

"Always nice to see a wiseass kid turn into a pillar of the community," he responded, his voice as insincere as Graywolf's. "So I guess when the tech completes the dump on Quintero's cell, we aren't going to find any calls from his phone to yours. Since you don't know him."

The kid's gaze flicked to the one-way glass at the far end of the interview room. "That phone wasn't mine, remember?"

"Yeah, so you said." Joe stared at him, letting the silence stretch and grow tense. Most people, especially people under stress, didn't like silence. There was a human compulsion to fill it, to maybe blurt out things they didn't mean to say, and later regretted.

But Graywolf slanted another glance at the one-way glass and clamped his lips, folding his hands on the table like a choirboy in prayer. "Is there anything else I can help you with?"

"I don't know. Is there?"

"Nope. Sorry." The chair scraped the floor as the kid pushed away from the table, stood. He picked up his jacket, which he'd hung carefully on the back of the chair. Like the rest of him, it looked expensive and useless. Shrugging into it, he gave Joe a nasty grin. "Heard you killed that guy. Quintero. How'd that feel?"

Joe stared at him, not responding. Their gazes did battle for a moment before the kid lifted a hand and sauntered to the door. Joe let him get halfway through it before saying, "Oh, Brant? I'll be in touch."

There was a hesitation in the kid's stride, just for a moment. Then without a backward glance he walked away.

Leaning forward, Joe reached for the tape recorder on the table and pressed the stop button. He was allowing it to rewind when Captain Tapahe came into the room. "What'd you think?" The captain had watched the entire interview from behind the one-way glass.

"I think if the kid's daddy had gotten wind that we were talking to him, he'd have been lawyered up before coming in here."

"His choice. I'm guessing he doesn't want his father involved unless absolutely necessary." Joe would be willing to place bets on it. Even a father's patience would be stretched to the breaking point with the scrapes the kid had been in the last few years. No, Brant Graywolf would try to handle this on his own as long as possible. "He won't alert the old man unless we get too close."

"Won't get anything from him then, either."

"No. So if the need arises, we'll play him another way." Brant Graywolf was a smug little SOB with a royalty's sense of entitlement. As long as he thought he was outsmarting the police, outsmarting Joe, he'd consider this all a game. Joe was perfectly willing to play. But he'd make the rules.

"Who's up next?"

"Mary Barlow. She was Quintero's main squeeze, so chances are she won't be feeling too cooperative, either."

The captain nodded. "Well, keep working through the list of his acquaintances. We should have the retrieved phone log by tomorrow, the next day at the latest."

Joe nodded and rose. "I didn't get any answer to the messages I left for Barlow so I'm going to her place."

"Want me to assign someone to ride along?"

He shook his head. If he knew Arnie, he'd be back before the ink dried on the doctor's release orders. It'd take him that long to bring someone new up to speed on the case. "I can handle it."

Tapahe waved him off. "Keep me posted."

Joe promised to do so, and the two men parted. But three hours later he was beginning to wonder if there'd be anything to report. Barlow was proving elusive. No one had answered at the run-down motel where she rented a room by the month. Nor had there been any sign of her at her sister's house across town. He'd checked out all the spots Barlow frequented, the list supplied grudgingly by her sibling, to no avail.

Although the sister denied it, he began to consider in earnest that the woman might have skipped town.

Her sheet wasn't as long as Quintero's, but she had priors. A couple solicitation charges and a misdemeanor for possession. There was no outstanding warrant for her, however, so there'd be no urgent need for her to leave. Unless she knew something.

Rather than chase after her any further, Joe drove back to the motel, parked his unmarked black Jeep a few doors down from Barlow's room and prepared to wait. Investigations were all about waiting. Arnie had once accused him of having the patience of a sphinx. Recently, though, thanks to his ex, even his patience was strained to the limit.

An hour and forty minutes later, a battered white Grand Am pulled into the slot in front of the nearby motel door. Even with her hair pulled up and wearing sunglasses, he recognized Mary Barlow from her mug shot. He let her get several feet from her car and start fumbling in her purse for her keys before he got out of the Jeep and approached her.

"Ms. Barlow?"

The woman whirled, her movement jerky and fraught with tension. "What? Who are you? What do you want?"

She was jittery with nerves, or something chemical. Joe forced his voice low and soothing. "Tribal police investigator Joseph Youngblood, ma'am." He drew out his ID and flipped it open as he stopped before her. "I have a few questions for you."

"I ain't talking to no *cop*. Especially after one of you killed Oree. You can all burn in hell. You hear me?" Her voice had gone shrill.

The sentiment was unsurprisingly similar to the one Quintero had verbalized yesterday. Joe tucked away his ID. "I thought it'd be easier for you to talk to me here. But we can go downtown if you'd prefer."

A bitter laugh escaped her. "What I'd prefer is for Oree to still be alive. He never hurt no one and the cops shot him in cold blood."

"Were you there?" His question seemed to catch her off guard. "How do you know how things went down?"

Her fingers clenched around her purse. "Didn't have to be there. I hear things. And I know how cops operate."

"And I have some questions about how Oree operated. Do you want to answer them here or inside?"

Barlow looked at the key in her hand, then shook her head, dropped it back in her purse. "I ain't letting you in my place. Don't have to, either. You don't got a warrant."

"No problem," he said mildly, surveying her. "We can talk out here. Tell me about your relationship with Oree."

When her thin lips tightened mutinously, he shrugged. "Or I can take you back to the station and we'll talk there. Makes no difference to me, if you've got the time."

He watched her struggle with that for several seconds before she folded her arms across the surgically enhanced chest straining against her skimpy belly shirt. "What do you wanna know?"

"You were his girlfriend?"

She sniffed. "Girlfriend. Mother. Sister. Priest. I was everything to Oree. He was a needy kind of guy, you know?"

"How much time did you spend together? Did you see him every day? Every night?" If she'd been around as much as Joe suspected, there was no way she could have avoided knowing about his drug involvement.

The same fact seemed to have occurred to her, as well. "I was around. But I had my own life, okay? I can't tell you much about what he did when I wasn't there. What time we had together we didn't spend talking."

He reached out, took the sunglasses off her face. She tried to swat his hand away, but he dodged the action, let the glasses dangle from his fingers. "I like to see who I'm speaking to." And he wanted to be able to tell if she was lying to him. "You knew he was involved in drugs."

She shook her head hard at his statement. "Uh-uh, no sir. I didn't know nothing about that, and you can't prove differently."

"No." He waited, saw the relief flicker across her face, then added, "Not yet, anyway. But we're rounding up all his clients and we'll be asking them about Oree. About you. Funny thing, when people think they're going down on a drug charge, they get real conversational. If you were there during any of the transactions, we're going to hear about it sooner or later."

She lifted a shoulder, the gesture as bored as her expression. He took a notebook out of his pocket, flipped it open. "You know any of these people?" He began reading off the names of Quintero's known acquaintances. Each name was punctuated with a short, "Nope," until he got to the name he'd purposefully left for last. Gaze on her face, he said, "How about Brant Graywolf. You know him?"

She ducked her head, her hand fishing in her purse, until she came up with her room key. Hefting the straps of her purse over her shoulder, she reached out and plucked the glasses from his hand, settling them on her nose. "No. I told you, I didn't mix in Oree's business. He didn't mix in mine. Now I got appointments and you're holding me up."

"What kind of business you in, Mary?"

"I'm a masseuse. Got my license and everything."

"What's your phone number?"

Suspicion registered in her expression. "Why?"

"Maybe I'll call for a massage someday. What's your number?" When the cell phone forensics came back on Quintero's, he wanted to be able to identify as many of the phone numbers as possible.

After she told him and he wrote it down, she unlocked her room door and stepped inside. "I've told you everything I know. I don't want you bothering me again."

Joe didn't respond, just stood and watched as she slammed the door. He heard the dead bolt snap into place on the other side. The only truths she'd revealed had all been nonverbal. Her heavily made-up eyes had been red and swollen. Perhaps her grief over Oree's death was genuine. As genuine as the emotion that had flashed across her face when he'd mentioned Graywolf's name.

Fear.

Chapter 7

When she heard the knock on her front door that morning, Delaney froze, certain for a moment it was Joe. Which didn't explain the crazy little spiral of heat that traversed from her belly to her chest, because she had her hormones, *all* her emotions, firmly under control now. A couple nights' sleep had done wonders for reestablishing the emotional distance that had served her well the last two years. And the fact that she hadn't seen or heard from Joe Youngblood since she'd given him those pictures hadn't hurt, either.

The knock sounded again, and something inside her eased. It was hard to imagine Joe knocking when her Jeep was parked out front. Up to this point, he hadn't exactly proved to be a staunch observer of etiquette.

"Miss Carson?"

It was also hard to imagine Joe ever addressing her in that openly flirtatious manner. The face of the man on the other side of her screen door was split in a wide grin. "Yes."

"I'm Edison Bahe. You can call me Eddie. The Tribal Council hired me as your guide."

Eddie Bahe was tall, whipcord lean, with strong white teeth that flashed in a perpetual smile. He also had a steady stream of patter that was nearly impossible to interrupt. "I know it's rather early in the morning but I was in the area and thought I'd stop and say hello. Just to introduce myself and maybe get an idea of your plans. What you want to see first. Where you want to go. President Taos put me at your disposal, ma'am."

When he paused to take a breath, Delaney unlatched the door and joined him on the porch. "I recognize your name." Charley had mentioned it at dinner the other night. "I thought we were scheduled to meet Saturday, but the details were left vague. Where do you suggest I start?"

"Well…" Eddie tipped his cowboy hat back, appeared deep in thought. "We're just fifty miles east of the Grand Canyon, eighty miles southwest of Monument Valley and seventy miles north of the San Francisco Peaks. You'll have to see Canyon de Chelly, of course, but you'll want to devote more time to it. It's about three hours from here. You might want to consider getting a camping permit before going there."

"I believe President Taos included one in the papers he sent along for me."

"The thing I'd recommend—" Eddie leaned a hand against the porch post "—is to start tomorrow instead of Saturday. We could go to Monument Valley real early and be back in time to hit the flea market in town. It'd be a touristy sort of thing, but would also be a great way for you to see lots of Navajo crafts and taste some home-cooked dishes."

Beneath Eddie's polished veneer, Delaney realized, beat a cash register for a heart. She smiled. "I didn't realize I needed a guide to get to the flea market."

His perpetual grin turned sheepish. "'Course you don't. But I do know which vendors have the best turquoise for the best value. And who sells the best-tasting corn cake."

It wouldn't hurt, she supposed, to take Eddie along that first time. She'd already learned that Navajos, through their clan system, had extensive family connections. Her first several weeks on the reservation would be spent making acquaintances and connections of her own. He might be able to facilitate that.

"All right, we'll start tomorrow," she decided. "But we'll do the flea market first, then if there's still time we'll head to Monument Valley."

His face lit up at the words. "That's fine with me. I'll pick you up at—"

"How about I pick you up," she interrupted him. With the equipment she'd be bringing, it'd be easier to pack her own vehicle.

He gave her a slow wink. "Never let it be said that

Eddie Bahe turned down a ride from a beautiful lady." He gave her directions to his house, which was located in one of the new housing developments just inside the city limits.

"Tomorrow morning, 9:00 a.m. sharp," she called after him, as he headed back toward his older model black Chevy pickup. "If you're not ready, you walk." He was in the truck, backing away from the house when she thought to add, "Rocky Mountain Time." She thought she saw his teeth flash one more time before he turned onto the road headed back to town.

Time was one thing she struggled with on Navajo Nation lands. The Navajo language had no word for it. And to make things more confusing, Tuba City was in two time zones, with half going by Rocky Mountain daylight saving time, sometimes called Navajo time, and the other half going by Rocky Mountain standard time. Meeting up with Eddie tomorrow morning could prove interesting.

She headed back into the house to shower and dress. She was scheduled to meet with Charley again that afternoon, as she had for the last few days. Mindful of Joe's warning, she had been careful to not stay for more than three or four hours at a time. It meant more frequent trips but Charley seemed to welcome the company and she certainly didn't mind. He was one of the most fascinating men she'd ever met, and completely irresistible.

Stripping off her clothes, she turned on the shower and stepped inside. But not before it occurred to her that the only man she'd met in years that she trusted absolutely was an eighty-year-old Navajo elder.

The irony wasn't lost on her.

Joe was finishing the report, compiling the conversations he'd had with Quintero's acquaintances that day. Balefully, he glared at the computer monitor as another phrase was underlined by the software program, indicating a problem with his spelling, sentence structure, or both. He was a cop, not a novelist. Arnie and he had a system. He could usually coax the other man into writing the reports, if he also let him drive when they were in the Jeep. It was tough to sit in the passenger seat day after day, especially given Arnie's driving ability, but it was far worse to type the endless reports at day's end.

He was still pecking away at the computer when he heard Vicki Smith, the office specialist, behind him. "Visitor for you, Joe."

Turning, he saw a slight, bespectacled man with fading blond hair and blue eyes. Bruce Glenn, his former father-in-law.

Warily he stood, shot a glance at Vicki, who merely raised her eyebrows and moved away. "Bruce."

"Joe. I hate to bother you at work. The thing is, I've called your house a few times and can't seem to find you at home. I thought I'd take a chance on catching you here."

"Is something wrong? With Heather? Jonny?" A parent's dread reared quickly. He'd just spoken to his son last night, and he'd seemed his usual exuberant self.

"No, no. Nothing like that."

Relief filtered through Joe and he noticed for the first time Garcia at her desk, diligently appearing as though she weren't listening. Several other officers were in the vicinity, as well. "Follow me." He led Bruce to the staff room, and stared at the lone occupant who was hovering hopefully over the coffee maker. After several seconds the man glanced up, looked from Joe to Bruce and excused himself.

When he'd left, Joe let the door shut behind him and faced Glenn. "What's on your mind, Bruce?" He'd always gotten along well enough with the man during his marriage to Heather. When they'd been dating, Bruce had made no bones about the fact that he didn't think Joe was good enough for his daughter, but then, no one would have lived up to his expectations for the girl he'd raised alone and, in Joe's estimation, spoiled beyond belief. She'd had an indulged childhood, with summers spent accompanying her father on ruin res-toration projects in the Yucatán and winter breaks skiing in Aspen. After the wedding, though, the man had been cordial, and he'd doted on Jonny since the boy's birth.

"Well, it's Heather, of course." Bruce took off his glasses and cleaned them on his shirt, a familiar absent-minded gesture of his. "I don't mind saying, it's tough for me, not having her and Jonny nearby. Especially in the summer, when I have more time on my hands." He'd taught history at Tuba City High for nearly thirty years now. "It can't be easy for you, either. Occasional weekends with the boy, when you were used to seeing him nearly every day."

As if the words had barbs, they arrowed deep into his chest. Twisted. Joe's jaw tightened. "No. It's not easy."

"Maybe you could do something to get her to return here." Bruce settled the glasses back on his nose and swallowed hard. "This situation…it's not good for any of us. It's got to be hard for Jonny to understand all the changes in his life recently. He needs his family around him at a time like this. All of his family."

It was hard to disagree. Jonny's home was here. His family was here, his grandfather and great-grandfather. His friends. Even the T-ball team he'd hoped to play on this summer. Heather had disrupted all that when she'd insisted on moving to Window Rock. She'd said she needed to find work. Joe remained unconvinced. She'd never worked a day in her life, and he was certain Bruce would have been glad to resume supporting her.

So that meant she'd done it solely to punish him. Maybe because he'd never been able to figure out how to make her happy. Probably because he'd finally gotten tired of trying.

"I don't know what I can do. The custody hearing date is set for three weeks from now. Until then we both have to wait."

"C'mon." Bruce shuffled his feet, tried for a smile. "You're a cop. You've got friends all over the reservation who are cops. You can make things… difficult for her, can't you? You could make her see it's better all around if she just comes home."

Joe eyed him narrowly. "I'm not quite sure what you're suggesting."

"What I'm suggesting is that you prove you love your son, even if you no longer love my daughter." His voice had risen with the statement, and Joe glanced at the closed door, wondering how many officers outside it were listening. "What I'm suggesting is that you use any means necessary to do what's best for Jonny. Or don't you care that your son is living among strangers? That you have to content yourself with every other weekend visits when you used to be a real part of his life?"

"Yes, I care." Joe kept his voice low, his anger held in check. "But I'm not going to pull some stupid stunt that will jeopardize my case when it gets to court. I don't like this situation any better than you do, but we both have to give this some time. It will sort itself out in the end." He had to believe that. Had to believe his lawyer's prediction of his chances in court. Because some days it was the only thing that kept him going.

Curious now, he looked more closely at the man. Bruce seemed thinner, a little stooped in the shoulders, and it was obvious that the situation was wearing on him, as well. "You've always had a close relationship with Heather. I can't believe she wouldn't listen to you if you tried to talk to her."

The man puffed out a breath. "Heather hasn't been listening to much I have to say for the last several months. I don't know where her head is, I really don't." He sighed, straightened. "Just…promise you'll think about what I said, Joe. Custody cases are never a sure thing. You may need to use other means to bring your son home."

Bruce reached for the doorknob and Joe stood aside, let him leave. It was probably the first time in Bruce's life that he hadn't gotten his daughter to do exactly as he wanted. Well, the second time, given that she'd married Joe. But clearly Bruce was desperate if he'd come here, begging Joe to…do what? Arrange some sort of private harassment for his ex? Kidnap his son?

Joe shook his head. Would his desperation reach Bruce's level if things didn't go his way in court? He didn't want to think about the complications that would arise should he be forced to transfer to be closer to his son. Charley was over eighty, and although he'd made it through the bypass surgery, he was at the age where he needed his family around him.

Deliberately, Joe closed the door on the staff room, trying to leave those thoughts behind, as well.

Captain Tapahe was waiting impatiently by his desk. "You've got a call, Joe." As his stride quickened, the man lowered his voice. "You can take it in my office. It's President Taos."

Joe strode into the other man's office, picked up the receiver. "This is Youngblood."

"Frank Taos, here, Joe. We've never met, but your captain has been singing your praises."

Warily, Joe looked up as the captain joined him in the office, closing the door behind him. "That's good to hear."

"I'm just checking on how you're coming on that incident involving Delaney Carson. I don't think I have to tell you just how delicate the matter is."

"I checked it out. The place was deserted, but it's clear there had been some sort of illegal activity there. Whoever fired those shots did it to scare her away from the operation."

"So your captain said." There was an expectant pause, but Joe had no idea what he was expected to say to fill it. "Have you talked to the owner yet?"

"Not yet." Apparently politicians had far more time on their hands than did tribal police investigators. "I'm in the middle of a multiagency drug investigation."

"Which I'm sure is a priority. But I wanted you to know that I consider the Carson incident a priority, too. I'd like you to give it your closest attention. Wouldn't hurt to keep an eye on the woman yourself, until we know for sure she's in no danger."

"I don't think that's necessary." At his captain's scowl, Joe added a belated, "Sir."

"And I think it is." The steel in the man's tone was unmistakable. "If you have too much on your plate I'm sure I can talk to some people, get you reassigned to free up more of your time. It's your call."

Joe held the receiver away from his ear in disbelief. Since when did the Tribal Council and Navajo President interfere with ongoing police investigations? Temper barely held in check, he said tightly, "That won't be necessary."

"Good. Keep me posted on what you discover. I can

tell you find this an imposition, but I appreciate your help in the matter."

Slowly, Joe dropped the phone back in its cradle and turned to face Captain Tapahe. The man shrugged. "I tried, Joe. He wanted me to pull you from the crystal ice case and I said no. This is give and take. Accept it at that."

"Accept it?" There was a low burn in the pit of his belly. "Accept that someone who knows nothing about our cases can just arbitrarily pull some strings and screw up months of investigation? When did politicians start interfering with our work?"

"Since longer than you realize." Tapahe rounded his desk and dropped heavily into the chair behind it. "We deflect as much of this kind of thing as we can, but you're stuck on this one. Just humor the man. You were continuing to look into the matter anyway, right? That's why you needed the information from the land bureau. Just follow up on that, get back to the president tomorrow and maybe that will be the end of it."

"I was going to talk to more of Quintero's customers today," Joe objected. "I have a list of them that Arnie and I put together. I might be able to squeeze one or two of them, get something more...."

"Give the list to Garcia. She can do it for you." At Joe's scowl he said, "It's called compromise, Youngblood. Be grateful you got a choice."

A choice? Joe swallowed the retort that rose to his lips and turned to leave the office. When it came to Delaney Carson, he'd already learned to leave his preferences out of the equation.

* * *

Delaney held her sandwich in one hand and clutched the edge of the open screen door with the other to survey the man glowering at her from her porch. "Now what? Did I kick a kitten? Swat a fly? Make a list of my offenses. I'll throw myself on the mercy of the court." He didn't crack a smile. Imagine that.

"You've got some pretty powerful friends."

She cocked her head, considering. "You think? Well, there's Joe Caprio at the McDonald's back home in Witchita. He always gives me extra fries with my order, but powerful?" She shook her head. "I wouldn't go that far." She let the door slam behind him as he strode into the living room.

His eyes glinted. "I'm not talking about some loser offering free fried food, I'm talking about Taos."

She blinked. "Navajo Nation President Taos? What about him?"

"Apparently he's concerned about you. Concerned enough that he threatened to have me reassigned from this drug investigation—the case my colleague and I have worked for months—just to be sure you're in no danger."

She eyed him warily. She'd seen him hostile before. Abrasive, even. But she didn't ever remember seeing him like this. It was like watching a bomb, waiting to detonate. She was pretty sure she didn't want to be around for the explosion. "I could call him," she offered tentatively. "Assure him that I feel perfectly safe…"

"That won't help. The only thing that's going to keep him happy is for me to clear the whole thing up in addition to my other ongoing cases. So c'mon. Let's get to it."

"C'mon...where?"

"To Cowboy Nahkai's place. I found out today that his family owns the land where you were shot at."

Excitement warred with trepidation. "You think he might be involved in whatever operation was being hidden out there?"

Joe finally looked at her, really looked. "Are you kidding? He's over ninety. And although he's still pretty spry, I doubt he's out cruising around on four-wheelers. He's probably leased his land to someone. And since he doesn't have a phone, we'll go out and ask him about it."

Delaney took a bite of her sandwich, chewed. "I still don't see where I come into this." She had work to do, photos to load and sort. Recordings to transcribe. The afternoon with Charley had been another treasure trove of information. She wanted to get it written while her notes were fresh.

She might not be above making excuses to avoid spending hours in his company. But tonight she didn't have to search for any. Unfortunately, she could tell from his expression that he was unswayed.

"You're coming along," he said firmly. His lips curved then, but it wasn't an especially friendly smile. "Taos wants me to look out for you. Apparently he thinks you need a babysitter. So for tonight I do that by dragging you along."

Delaney stared at him, weighing her options. She didn't especially want to be *dragged* anywhere. Not to mention her vow to spend as little time with him, near temptation, as possible.

On the other hand, he wasn't especially tempting when he was this crabby, so her hormones should be safe enough. And she did feel somewhat responsible for his dilemma, since she knew what long hours he'd been putting in.

Both on the job and off it, a sly inner voice whispered.

"Okay. Let me get my shoes."

If he was surprised by her capitulation, he didn't show it. Instead he was eyeing her sandwich with a decidedly avaricious look in his eye. "Do you have any more of those?"

She looked up from the bright pink flip-flops she was slipping on. "None that would fit you."

He did that thing with his lips, pointed them toward her sandwich and little sparks of awareness flickered to life under her skin as she focused on his mouth. It really was beautifully formed. Full chiseled lips, that looked hard but were surprisingly soft to kiss. Until their desire had torched them both and then his mouth had turned fierce, hungry, whipping her passion to a fever pitch.

Delaney drew in a shaky breath and headed toward the kitchen. "I can make more." The key, she told herself, as she took out the ham and bread, was to stop focusing on his lips except to keep him talking. She rarely had trouble resisting him when he was ordering her around.

* * *

Cowboy Nahkai had a seamed weathered face and a slight body that looked more wiry than fragile. Although it was barely seven o'clock, they caught him as he'd been about to turn in.

"I get up at four every morning. Have for most of my life. It's a habit I don't like to break."

Although he invited them in, they ended up sitting on his front porch, facing what promised to be a truly spectacular sunset in another hour or so. The horizon was already rosy, as if blushing in anticipation.

"I want to thank you, Mr. Nahkai, for your hospitality." Delaney sipped from her mug of Navajo coffee. "I understand you're one of those who generously gave permission for me to travel freely on your property."

"If you are to capture the beauty of our land, you must be able to see it," he said simply. "The land has withstood much. It certainly will withstand some pictures. Have you had a chance to explore this area yet?"

Before she could answer, Joe put in smoothly, "She plans to, but she's only been in town a few days. She wanted me to bring her out here so she could familiarize herself with the drive. And also to check if there's anyone who will be bothered by her roaming the area. You're in pretty good shape, but I assume you're not still running sheep yourself."

The older man cackled. "It's been a while since I chased after a flock. No, I've leased most of the land for years. Phillip Roanhorse had it for a long time, but he sold his livestock a few years back and retired."

Delaney sat back and let Joe direct the conversation. She wasn't sure why he didn't want Nahkai to learn of the incident on his property, but she was willing to let him handle it.

"That's right, I know Phillip. He used to whittle whistles for me when I was a boy and he'd come to visit Grandfather. I'd forgotten he retired." Joe brought the mug of coffee to his lips, drank. "Who did you say holds the lease now?"

The old man frowned, as if trying to think. "I'd have to look it up. William has taken care of my lease agreements for the last couple years. I don't get involved anymore. He's been a good help since he's come back. His dark spirit is gone, and he's recovered his *hozho*."

Joe went still, his eyes predatory. Delaney glanced at the older man to see if he'd noticed, but he continued to sip his coffee.

"I didn't know William was out." Joe's voice was amazingly even. "Is he around? I'd like to say hello."

Nahkai waved a hand. "He is probably out back with the cars. If you find him, tell him to come join us. He probably doesn't even realize we have guests."

Rising to his feet, Joe cradled the mug in one hand and headed to the porch steps. "I'll do that."

William Nahkai did, indeed, have his head under the hood of a new truck in the well-equipped garage out back. Joe looked around, noting the changes that had taken place on the property since he'd last been there, years earlier. He wondered cynically how many of them had been made because of this man's penchant for squandering his grandfather's money.

"William." He watched with satisfaction as the man threw an impatient look over his shoulder, then abruptly paled when he recognized Joe. "You weren't gone nine years. Get out early for good behavior?"

The other man snatched up a grease rag, twisted it in his hands as he turned to face Joe. "Hey, Joe." His smile looked more like a grimace. "Yeah, I've been out for a couple years." Seconds ticked by. "Good to see you again."

Joe leaned against the truck's bumper. "I hear you're taking care of all Cowboy's business. Didn't recall you cared much for that sort of thing."

"Things are different now. *I'm* different." William worked diligently at scrubbing the grease off his hands. "I finally got that it's all about family, you know? So I'm looking out for Grandfather. Everyone else is too far away and I'm not married or anything." He lifted a shoulder. "It's working out well enough."

Looking meaningfully at the new truck, Joe said, "Looks like it." While the other man flushed, he continued, "You're taking care of the lease agreements now? So maybe you can tell me who holds the lease on the northern part of the property. Where those buttes and caves are."

William managed a laugh. "Lots of areas like that on Cowboy's property, Joe."

"This is a half hour off the highway. Dirt road that's barely a path runs north and south parallel to it."

"I've got three or four lessees these days. I'd have to look it up, see if I can figure out where you mean."

Joe nodded. "You could do that. You could even send me to track down the leaseholders and ask them all the same questions, but you know what, William? *I* haven't changed in the last few years. I still get down-right mean if I think someone's jerking me around. So if I do go to all the trouble of questioning those people, just to find out that maybe none of them hold the lease to the piece of property I'm interested in, I'm going to be unhappy." He watched the other man swallow hard, "Then I'm going to come back. And when I do, you'll join your grandfather and me for a little discussion about what the hell you've been doing with his land."

"I didn't do anything wrong," William said sullenly. "You don't need to go making trouble and upsetting Grandfather."

"Just what is it that you didn't do?"

The other man threw a quick glance toward the house. "I leased all the land. And every dime is accounted for, every penny."

"Okay." Joe gave a slow nod. "So let's go back to the house and you can get me the names and contact infor-mation of those you leased it to."

William didn't move. "Thing is—" he swallowed "—that parcel you mentioned…it's not much good for running sheep. I didn't see the difference if I leased it out separate. Got an extra few thousand for it, and that's more than I'd have gotten if I'd bundled it with the other acres, the way it used to be. I mean, what's the harm?"

"The name?"

"I don't know. Some guy approached me at the flea market, right after I'd gotten out. Seemed to know who I was. He wanted to rent that part of the property and enough surrounding land that he'd have some privacy."

"For what?"

"He didn't say and I didn't ask." His voice had gone from whiny to mulish. "Nothing illegal about what I did. I don't have to ask why he wanted it. As long as he sends his money in on time, that's all that matters to me."

Joe took the drawing out of his pocket that Delaney had started and the composite artist at headquarters had finished. "Do you recognize this man? Is he the one who approached you?"

William leaned forward to study the picture. "I couldn't say for sure. It was almost two years ago, and I never saw him again. He just sends a money order to an account I set up in Phoenix. That's all the contact I have with him. He wanted me to stay clear of the property and it's not like that was a hardship. It's out in the middle of nowhere."

"And that didn't tip you off because all your lessees request that, right?" Disgusted, Joe folded up the picture and shoved it in his pocket.

"So, what'd he do? I mean..." William shuffled his feet when Joe looked at him. "Why are you hunting for him?"

"Well, attempted murder, for one thing." Given the shots the man had fired at Delaney, Joe didn't figure he'd have trouble making that charge stick. "I'm not sure yet what he was up to on your grandfather's property. But you'd better start hoping that whatever dirt he was into doesn't come back to splash on you. I understand parole officers aren't too forgiving about things like that."

Chapter 8

"You and Cowboy seemed to be getting along well." Joe shot a look at Delaney across the interior of the Jeep. "I've never known him to be that open with strangers."

"It's my midwestern charm. Few men can resist it."

"Maybe it's the other way around. I've heard stories. Back in the day, I hear he was quite a ladies' man. Been married three times. Outlived them all."

She scooched down in the seat and braced her knees against the glove compartment. "You didn't tell me he was a shaman. A crystal gazer, he said. He invited me back to talk to him. I'll definitely make a point of doing that."

Changing the subject, she asked curiously, "So what did you find out from…William, was it?"

Joe nodded, the sunglasses he wore shielding his

eyes. "Cowboy's grandson. Seems ol' Billy worked himself a private deal with someone a couple years ago. He claims he leased that section of land to some stranger who approached him. Only saw him the once and can't give a description of him."

"Convenient," she muttered. "Do you believe him?"

It took a while for Joe to answer. "For now, anyway. William was sent up for operating a chop shop in Flagstaff. He'd steal a vehicle, disassemble it and sell the parts. Strictly small-time. Maybe had another guy or two working with him when he was busted. Had the bad luck of stealing the mayor of Flagstaff's new Porsche."

"But you found lots of tracks at the site, you said."

"Probably a pickup, and at least one large van or panel truck. ATVs. But nothing that would lead me to believe William was operating in that area. Why would he? He's got it made now, living a pretty easy life for very little work, just pretending to take care of Cowboy."

Delaney frowned. She didn't like the idea of the remarkable man she'd just met being taken advantage of, even by family. "I think you should have brought him in," she said firmly. "Put a scare in him at least."

He threw her an amused glance. "So now you're Miss-demeanor?"

She made a face. "He might know something. Maybe if you had that picture I started for you, the one you were going to..." A folded-up paper landed in her lap. Unfolding it, she studied the composite the police artist had completed. "So now what?"

"Our mug files have been computerized for a few

years now. I'll feed in a composite sketch and the computer compares it to the mug shot database, using a standard composite program. I just haven't had time to sit down with it."

When she made an impressed sound, one corner of his mouth curved. "Our federal tax dollars at work. Someone wrote a grant. Yet we still have a hard time getting radios that work and run-flat tires for the police vehicles."

"So when do you think that you'll get around to matching the sketch?"

"You're as bad as Taos," he muttered. "I could go back and do it tonight. I'm getting used to going without sleep."

"You don't have to do that," she responded mildly. She waited a beat. "Tomorrow will be soon enough." Laughing at his expression, she continued, "I've got a date tomorrow with the guide the council was kind enough to provide me with. The way I understand it, I can use him for any tour I want to take on Navajo Nation lands, which will make things a lot easier for me."

"Like I said, you've got a powerful friend. Taos is protecting his investment."

His tone hardened with the last statement, and Delaney glanced at him curiously. "Taos? What investment?"

"You can't afford to be naive. The council bucked a lot of public resentment by bringing a non-Navajo in here to write a book on our culture that could have been done by a tribe member."

So they were back to that again. Straightening, she set her feet on the floor. "Forgive me for believing that my experience in photojournalism and my résumé can't be duplicated, despite my lack of bloodline."

There was impatience in the look he threw her, but something else, as well. Something that may have been concern. "That's right, it can't be duplicated. They're using you, Delaney. Banking on the publicity your next project is going to bring, counting on the fact that the publishing world is going to pay major money to snap up anything you decide to write, and that millions of readers are going to want to get their hands on it."

Lifting a shoulder, she wondered at the tinge of bitterness in his words. "That's the way my world works, Joe. You spend years clawing and scratching, hoping to get to this point. If you're fortunate, you get there through sheer talent, but there are lots of people in the field just as talented, just as driven. So sometimes circumstances, or sometimes just dumb luck, lands a person at the top. In the end it doesn't matter how I got here because now publishers are calling my agent, not the other way around. Of course the council is looking at the money and publicity this project stands to bring the tribe. Anyone who hires me at this point in my career is banking on the same thing."

"And how will the publicity affect you?"

Puzzled, she turned in her seat to face him. "What do you mean?"

The look he gave her was grim. "I know how the press works. There will be…what do you call them, book tours? And interviews?"

"If my agent and publicist do their jobs, yes."

"And the interviewers won't just talk about your newest project, they'll drag up your experiences in Baghdad, rake up the past. Why would you willingly put yourself in that situation? Don't try to tell me it isn't going to bother you. I've seen just how powerful those memories are, remember."

There was a spurt of anger at the reminder. Yes, he'd seen her weak and vulnerable, and he'd never realize just how deeply that sliced. No one, not even her family, had ever known how close to the precipice she'd been at times, how little it would have taken to send her toppling over the edge.

Delaney didn't speak until she could be certain her voice would be steady. "I can handle that when it happens. Maybe you don't believe it, but I'm stronger, a lot stronger, than you give me credit for." He didn't have to know about the demons that still lingered in the night or her despair at recently realizing that she was not nearly as close to vanquishing them as she'd believed. "I don't fault the council for wanting to cash in on all the publicity my name can bring them. They made a good business decision, the right one for all concerned."

"Was it?" There was a bite to his words. "So who's concerned about you, Delaney? Who's looking out for what's best for you?"

Stunned, she could only stare at him. She'd thought this conversation had stemmed from his disagreement with the council's decision. But now…she could almost believe he sounded worried. About her.

Dusk was falling. He reached up to take off the dark glasses, folded them and stuffed them with just a little more force than necessary into place on the visor. "Just don't pretend that this won't cost you anything. Not with me."

Something unfurled in her chest and her lips curved. "Well, Joe Youngblood. Careful, or you'll have me thinking you're concerned on my behalf." The look he shot her was dangerous, but she just settled back, enjoying the crazy glow spreading through her system.

And it was crazy, she acknowledged freely. Crazy to be attracted to a man with whom there was no future. They had no connection, other than a chemistry that sparked to life every time they were together for more than a few minutes.

She'd seen a therapist for months when she returned to the States. He accused her of trying to exert control over her world because events in it had so rapidly rendered her helpless. Maybe he was right. Maybe she was seeing complications where none existed.

Despite what Joe thought, she was very, very good at protecting herself. But that didn't mean she didn't appreciate his showing a little protectiveness on her behalf.

The rest of the ride was accomplished in silence. But when Joe pulled up in front of her house and placed the vehicle in Park, Delaney slid toward him, slipped a hand along his jaw and pulled his head down to hers.

She could feel the surprise in him, the sudden tension that spoke of wariness or something else. She didn't try to identify it.

His inaction lasted only seconds. Then his mouth came alive beneath hers, and he pulled her closer, wrapping his arms around her. His dark, sensual flavor arrowed through her system, played havoc with her pulse.

When his tongue pushed into her mouth, she met it with her own. Her fingers delved into his hair and she brought him closer. He knew exactly how to kiss, she thought dizzily, hard, hot and wet, as if he was staking a claim. He exuded a smoldering sexuality that a woman couldn't help but want to test. And once tested, come back for more.

She unbuttoned the first three buttons of his denim shirt, then swept her hand in, fingers tingling where they touched warm smooth flesh. One of his hands came up to clasp hers, and slowly, reluctantly she opened her eyes.

"Hard to keep this straight. Are we done being smart?" he rasped.

Remembering their last conversation when she'd sent him away, she pressed a kiss to the side of his mouth. "How about if we settle for being careful?" He didn't respond, just continued to look at her with that heavy-lidded gaze. "I'm going to be here for several months, Joe. And then I'll leave. There's really no reason to deny ourselves this, is there?" She took his bottom lip in her teeth, scored it lightly. "As long as we both want the same thing until then, what's the harm?"

There was a long moment when she thought he'd

answer. But then the moment passed and he opened his car door, her hand still in his. Fingers clasped, they walked up her front stairs, the sexual awareness growing with every step.

Delaney fumbled for the keys she'd slipped in her pocket, opened the door. Already she was having second thoughts. Who was she kidding here, really, herself or Joe? But before the thoughts could take root and doubt bloom, he followed her in the doorway and crowded her against the wall, his mouth in search of hers again.

Her muscles took on the consistency of warm wax. There was the hunger she remembered in his kiss. The hint of savagery that called to an answering wildness in her. She'd never been one to shy away from danger. And there was danger of a sort in Joe's arms, in the fierce pressure of his mouth, in the dark promise of his touch. But it was a danger she longed to explore.

His hand went beneath her shirt, unsnapped her bra and she gave a hum of approval as she made short work of the rest of the buttons on his shirt, eager to feel flesh against flesh.

Their hands battled as they strove to undress each other and then he was pressed against her. She hissed in a satisfied breath at the contact. Her hands roamed his back, muscle punctuated by vertebrae, then traced the corded strength in his shoulders. His chest was smooth, his bronzed skin several shades darker than her own. And she had a slightly primitive compulsion to taste it with lips and tongue.

He shuddered against her when she did and Delaney had a moment to savor his reaction before she found herself swung up in his arms. His eyes glinted down into hers. "The bed this time."

Lazily, she linked her arms around his neck. "We found the bed last time," she reminded him. "Eventually."

He dropped her on the bed, his face stamped with unmistakable male appreciation as he swiftly stripped, modesty obviously not a factor. And he definitely had no cause to be modest. Delaney propped herself on one elbow to admire his hard flat abs, lean flanks and the straining length of his manhood.

Her perusal was cut short when he joined her on the bed. Her hands streaked over him, down his sleek ridged sides, around to clutch at his taut buttocks.

He had her naked in a few swift movements, then she pushed at his shoulders, urged him on to his back. A satisfied smile curving her lips, she slid on top of him, and savored for a moment the exquisite sensation of bare flesh to bare flesh everywhere they touched—legs, hips, chests.

There was something fundamentally sexy about a man who let a woman enjoy his body, slowly, languorously, without attempting to take control or hasten toward the end. She kissed the cord at the side of his neck, tested it with her teeth, before moving lower to explore the dips and hollows where sinew met bone. She teased one hard male nipple with her tongue. Her palm slid along his side, over his hip, across his belly, and she felt the muscles jump and clutch under her touch.

His hands were hard, just shy of rough, as they swept

over her shoulders to find her breasts. Her vision blurred as he took a nipple between thumb and forefinger, squeezing lightly. As a result her nip to the skin just above his hip was a bit sharper than she intended. But the resulting hiss she heard from him wasn't one of pain.

He was hard, turgid and she pressed her mouth along his belly, careful not to touch him where he straining and ready with anything more than a whisper-soft breath. Her fingers skated down a solid muscled thigh, nails scraping lightly and she could tell the exact moment when his patience neared its end.

The fingers he threaded through her hair were just short of desperate as her palm skated closer, inch by infinitesimal inch, until she closed her fingers around his rigid length. The satisfied sound he made abruptly strangled when she took him into her mouth.

She had mere moments to relish the flavor of him, infinitely dark and sinful, to slide her tongue down his velvety shaft and up again to taste the heated drop of his desire at the tip. To stroke him in a way designed to create a madness in his blood, a frantic hammering that would echo the tattoo of her own pulse.

He drew her up for a long desperate kiss, teeth and tongue clashing, his fingers wrapped in her hair, cupping the back of her head to hold her close. And she knew then that her efforts to drive him just a little mad entrapped her as well. In seducing, she was seduced. Her ministrations had the blood chugging through her veins, inflaming her passion even as she deliberately stoked his.

She felt him tense below her and knew that in another instant he'd have her stretched out beneath him. But she wasn't ready for it to be over. Not until they both were shuddering with desperation. Not until she'd etched a lasting memory on his mind, one that time and distance wouldn't completely erase, even after she was gone.

She tore her mouth from his and straddled him, her hands stroking his sweat-slicked skin. His clever wicked fingers were finding all the places guaranteed to make her forget everything but the urgent need to find the shattering satisfaction she already knew he could bring her.

He was fumbling with the foil packet he must have taken from his jeans pocket, cursing viciously when it took too long to open. Delaney took the latex sheath from him, positioned it and then rolled it with excruciating slowness down his shaft.

His face was a hard mask of desire, brutal in its intent. The sight called to something reckless in her, a fervent wish to tempt and tease until his uncertain control shattered. But his hands were on her breasts, the deliberate teasing of her nipples firing a path straight to her womb. He rose to take one in his mouth, not quite gently, and her vision hazed.

She pressed him back, guiding his hands over his head to close his fingers around the old iron headboard. His eyes slitted as she took him in her hand and guided him to her softness. Then paused until he gasped a curse, a prayer, before taking him in, one tiny fraction at a time.

He felt thick, huge. That first bolt of pleasure had her head lolling, breathing growing strangled. She took him farther inside and then, when she heard him groan, lifted again. She drove them both a little crazy by keeping her movements shallow, denying them both the urgent motion they craved.

Somewhere in the distance she heard an animal's mournful cry and the sound called to something basic in her, an elemental primal need to mate. She opened her eyes, tried to focus. Joe's face was sheened with sweat, his hands clutching tightly around the worn painted iron. Every muscle in his torso, his biceps and shoulders stood out in stark relief. She leaned forward, closed her teeth against one rock-hard pec and unleashed the beast.

In an instant his hands streaked to clutch her hips, and he jerked upward, impaling her on his length, seating himself fully, deeply inside her. Bracing her hands on the muscled planes of his chest she sat up and took over the motion, meeting the rhythmic pumping of his hips with wild frantic movements of her own.

The pleasure careened and collided through her system. Nothing else existed. There was only his slick muscles beneath her fingers, clenching and releasing with each movement, their harsh mingled breathing, the tight grip he had on her hips and the incredible full sensation of his possession.

His hand slipped between their bodies to fondle her, rubbing the sensitive bundle of nerves until need fisted tightly in her belly. His hips slammed against hers, in wild shuddering lunges, until the implosion of her climax tore through her.

And through the fog of her release she thought she heard her name on his lips, a low guttural sound as he followed her headlong into pleasure.

"I knew it," Joe muttered, scanning the list of incoming and outgoing numbers Lucas Tallhorse had managed to get from his exam of Quintero's cell phone. Looking up, he said, "Good job. I appreciate you getting to this so quickly."

"No problem. It was locked with a security code, but that was made easier by the fact that there are only a couple carriers available around here." Lucas animatedly explained how he'd gotten the information and Joe could feel his eyes begin to glaze. He listened to talk about SIM cards, IMEI and ESN numbers and digital communication protocols. Finally the man seemed to wind down. "They teach law enforcement classes on cellular forensics now." His broad face took on the wistful look a man usually reserved for an unattainable woman. "If I could take one, I'd probably get even better at it."

Joe's attention was back on the two typed pages stapled together. "Yeah? Maybe you should write a grant. Get the money that way."

"Hey, that's a good idea, Joe. I might do that." Tallhorse walked away, still talking. "A grant. Huh. I could do that."

But Joe had ceased listening. Graywolf, the little scumbag, was in this thing up to his lying teeth. Joe flipped through the pages, counting twelve calls from Quintero's cell to Graywolf's, and more than twice that many from Graywolf's to the dealer, all in a three-month period.

There were nineteen different numbers in all. He pulled out his notebook, found the page where he'd written Mary Barlow's number. Comparing it to the ones on the sheet, he found that calls to and from Barlow accounted for a full third of the ones on the list. Then he went back over the sheet and double-checked the numbers from the contact information he had on Quintero's known clients. When he was done, there were still several numbers unaccounted for. But only two of them showed up several times a month. It would be interesting to see if those two numbers would have shown up on Graywolf's cell, as well.

Joe sat back, considered. Where did Graywolf figure on the food chain here? Had he been selling drugs for Quintero? That seemed unlikely. Navajo Nation lands were small, relatively speaking. And chances were Quintero would not have wanted to share the wealth.

Which meant that Graywolf was connected to Oree in some other way, or that he was a step above Quintero in the same organization.

Joe considered the idea, decided it had merit. From what he could determine, Graywolf was working at a low-level job for his father's construction company. Would he be happy making an hourly wage after the kind of money he used to pull down dealing drugs?

They had focused their investigation on Quintero,

hoping he could lead them to his supplier, the one in charge of the pipeline smuggling drugs in from Mexico. At this point they had no other suspects.

But Joe had a whole lot of suspicion regarding Graywolf. And however Graywolf was involved in this thing, Quintero's death meant either an opportunity or a problem. Either way, Graywolf would be unable to remain inactive.

He was going to need a couple officers to help with surveillance on the punk. And they were going to have to do it in a way that would avoid having the kid's old man bring a mob of lawyers down here and close the kid off.

Glancing at the captain's door, Joe saw he was on the phone. While he waited for the captain to get free, he went to the computer and brought up the software program he'd told Delaney about. Scanning in the composite picture, he typed in the commands to have it provide a match to the sketch and sat back to wait.

Delaney had been sleeping soundly when he left her this morning, well before dawn. Even in slumber she didn't appear completely at ease, curled in a ball facing away from him, as if unused to sharing a bed with another. She was going to have to get used to it.

Just a few months and then she'd walk away. She'd made that clear enough. And it was what he wanted, too. Exactly what he wanted. No ties. No pretending the relationship meant more than it did.

And if the thought of that day had his chest tightening, his thoughts darkening, it was because he hadn't had his fill of her yet. Hadn't unlocked all the secrets that he sensed she was still hiding. He could only wonder if a few months was going to be long enough.

"In my next life, I want to be a special investigator. Lots of desk work. Probably drink coffee all day." FBI agent Delmer Mitchell leaned over his shoulder to peer at the computer screen. "You aren't downloading porn, are you?"

"Of course. I always do it at work because we have a faster connection here." Rising, he surveyed the fed. "You look like... hell."

"If it makes you feel better, I feel worse than I look. Where can we talk?"

Joe checked the staff room, found it empty and motioned him in. The man placed his briefcase on the table and sank into a chair. "I am getting too old for this job, or the victims are getting too young. Either way, it's been a helluva few weeks."

Multiagency cooperation had been key to the case Joe and Arnie had been assigned. The DEA was working the undercover drug connections and the FBI had been brought in to cover the felony aspect. The NTP had focused on the local angle, with the hope that by comparing information they would more quickly stop the supply of ice to the reservation, before the problem spiraled out of control.

That hope had been extinguished when the three young men were found murdered and their bodies dumped at the side of a road. The FBI had quickly claimed jurisdiction in the case while Joe and Arnie concentrated on the supplier of the drug found in the boys' systems. That investigation had led to Quintero.

"So what have you got?" Joe asked bluntly. This was the first time Mitchell had surfaced since Quintero's shooting, and if Joe had to guess, he'd say the agent had slept in the same rumpled suit since.

"Murder weapon was a 9 mm. Hasn't been found. Same weapon was used on all three. The road was a secondary scene, which we'd already figured." Joe nodded. There had been almost no blood at the site where the bodies were dumped, indicating they'd been shot elsewhere and then transported.

Mitchell opened his briefcase. He showed Joe some close-ups of the victims' knees. "Examination of their clothing and bodies indicates that they were forced to kneel for some time prior to their deaths, with their hands tied behind them. Maybe to plead for their lives."

Joe frowned, studying the pictures of abraded skin. "Sounds even more like gang-style killings."

"Or some gangsta wannabes. We've discovered the three didn't necessarily hang together, except to get high. Hosteen would score the drugs and the others paid him."

"So Hosteen could have been a little bigger than you think. Maybe he encroached on someone else's territory."

Mitchell looked doubtful. "C'mon, he was only sixteen. How big could he have gotten?"

"Maybe he owed money? Didn't pay his dealer so they were shot and dumped at a public place as a lesson to others?" Joe's voice was doubtful. That bespoke of the kind of savagery that was foreign to this area. Not unheard of. But still uncommon.

When drugs were involved, however, violence escalated alarmingly. One statistic estimated that as many as twelve percent of the Navajo teens were using meth. And with the purer form of ice showing up in the area, the brutality was bound to rise significantly.

"Anything else in the tox reports?"

"No, just that they'd all smoked ice a few hours before death."

Joe nodded. "Did any of them carry cell phones?" When Mitchell shook his head, he pressed, "What about landlines? Do you have phone records for Hosteen?"

"Right here." The agent produced a sheaf of paper. Joe rose and went back to his desk to get the stapled pages Tallhorse had prepared. Rejoining Mitchell, he looked up the Hosteen number and found it listed three times on the phone's incoming records. Six outgoing calls had been made from Quintero to Hosteen.

Mitchell linked his fingers and cracked his knuckles loudly. "Those six calls from Quintero to Hosteen might mean you're on the right track about him not paying. Is this Quintero's pattern?"

Joe slowly shook his head. "Never has been. I've heard of him beating a man half to death over a territorial dispute, but from all accounts he was high when he did it. But then, Oree appears to have gotten much bigger than he used to be. Maybe his tactics changed."

"Or someone else is pulling his strings. Find a gun when you tossed his place?"

"Two rifles."

"Well—" Mitchell gathered up the pictures and documents and placed them back in the case "—keep me posted. The trail on those homicides is going cold fast."

He stood and walked to the door. With his hand on the knob, he turned back. "Oh, I meant to tell you…saw your ex and your son when I was called back to the Phoenix field office yesterday. Cute kid. Thought you told me they were in Window Rock."

Joe stilled. "Phoenix," he repeated carefully.

"Recognized them from the picture you used to have on your desk. I was at Kmart because I forgot toothpaste again. Do that every time." He waved a hand. "Anyway. Heard your ex giving the clerk her new address for a check she was cashing. Wilshire Heights Boulevard…" He shrugged, continued out the door. "Doesn't matter. Could have sworn you said they were in Window Rock, though."

Joe followed him out the door, his limbs feeling wooden. "They were. They…moved again."

"I figured. Well, keep in touch. I'll do the same." Lifting a hand in farewell, Mitchell walked away, leaving Joe staring after him, thoughts fragmented. He didn't for a moment consider that Mitchell was mistaken. He'd seen that picture on Joe's desk at least a dozen times over the years, before it had been replaced with one of Jonny alone. And how many blondes did one see with a young Navajo boy in tow?

Rage seethed, a scalding tide threatening to overflow. Heather had lied to him. The knowledge pounded in his blood, hammered in his brain. If she was living off the reservation, without telling him, he could only conclude one thing. She was poised to take off with his son if the custody agreement didn't go her way.

His fists curled so tightly that his nails bit into his palms. She had to realize that tribal law was going to award custody of a Navajo child to a tribe member living on the land. She stood a chance of sharing custody if she remained on the reservation.

She stood no chance of custody off it.

Had Bruce known this yesterday when he'd come to visit? Had his odd request been an oblique warning that Heather was planning to whisk Jonny away from both of them?

With effort, Joe tamped down the mingled temper and fear that threatened to divert logic. After a moment of weighing options, he headed to the phone on his desk, to the list of contacts in the side drawer. Then calmly, coldly, he dialed the number of a private investigation firm in Phoenix.

Chapter 9

The flea market was a riot of the senses. Delicious smells wafted from some of the vendors' booths, while the brightly colored blankets, artwork and crafts caught the eye in others. There was a steady hum of voices, mingled, indistinguishable from this distance, except for an occasional burst of laughter.

Already Delaney's fingers itched for her camera, ready to capture the vivid color, the slivers of culture and the individuals whose very faces had stories to tell.

"I'd recommend an earlier start next time," Eddie advised. He'd insisted on carrying one of her tripods, and wore the strap of her second camera around his neck. "That's the only way to beat the heat in the summer months, at least for a while."

"I suppose." Although the statement was true, it didn't fill her with any enthusiasm. Sleep didn't come easily enough for her to voluntarily rouse from it only a handful of hours later. But waiting until sheer exhaustion overcame her, usually around 2:00 or 3:00 a.m., she could avoid the nightmares that often plagued her.

Last night had been an exception, however. She quickened her step to keep pace with Eddie's longer stride. The reason for her wakefulness had been the man lying beside her.

She'd been too aware of him. Long after passion had been spent and his breathing had gone deep, her senses remained alert. It still felt foreign to have his big body spread out next to hers, the weight of his arm curled around her waist, holding her close. Not unpleasant. Just…different.

It wasn't as if she'd never shared a bed with a man before. But she divided her life into two distinct parts, before Baghdad, and after. There'd been no one since Reid, no one since her life had snapped, then been put back together, forever altered. Sometimes she felt as though she'd been rendered blind two years ago, and she now had her hands out in front of her, feeling her way through days and experiences that used to come so effortlessly.

So when her instinct had been to roll away and curl up in a tight ball meant to ward off the specters that frequently accompanied sleep, she'd made herself lie there. And get used to the still steady warmth of a man she couldn't say she really even knew, on a personal level. But one who called to something deep inside her.

"Give me a minute." Delaney took the camera out of the case and shot the scene from where she stood, hoping to capture the bustle of human life. She clicked several pictures in quick succession, moved to take up a different position and started again. She wasn't sure how long it was before she grew aware of Eddie standing nearby, watching the throngs of people.

"Sorry." She straightened, sheepish. "I'm afraid there's going to be a lot of standing around when you're with me."

"I'm flexible." He gave her a broad grin. "That's why the council hired me. Plus I've worked as a guide at just about all the major tourist spots around these…" He broke off to tip his hat up to better view a woman, early twenties or so, walking by with a tray of breads. When he looked back at Delaney, saw her raised eyebrows he laughed without a shred of embarrassment. "I'm also a trained observer."

They fell in step again. "Then you observed that she was way too young for you."

"You think?" He gave her a flirtatious wink. "But you're not, are you?"

"I'm too old." They were probably close to the same age in years, but she couldn't match Eddie's laid-back manner. She'd never again be that open, that casual, that relaxed. But those same traits made him an easy companion. He stopped when she wanted to, making introductions to anyone he knew, which seemed to be more than half of the people they encountered. Most were cordial, inquisitive about her, although there were a few whose expressions went blank and closed at the introduction.

Delaney quickly found herself losing track of time, as she stopped by vendors and got wrapped up in conversation. One woman explained at length how she wove the brightly colored rugs she displayed and what the figures on them symbolized. She was more than happy to pose for some photographs when Delaney asked, and even agreed to talk to Delaney at a later date, when they'd have more time to discuss the craft she'd learned from her grandmother before her.

There were booths displaying old items rather than new, and Eddie explained that some of the vendors engaged in what would most accurately be called a swap meet. Others sold used goods, and business seemed to be brisk.

As promised, Eddie eventually led her to the booth with "the best" corn cakes and while he wrangled good-naturedly with the pretty girl selling them, Delaney stepped a little ways away and took more pictures. The crowd was thinning a bit, the sun merciless overhead. She caught sight of a little girl, no more than three or four, and she smiled, enchanted when the child grinned in return.

Delaney indicated her camera. "Would you like to take a picture?" The girl swiftly turned to check with her mother, who was on the other side of the booth straightening the turquoise necklaces and rings. At the woman's nod the child scampered over. Delaney helped her cradle the camera, showed her how to look through the optical viewfinder and take a picture of her mother before she straightened and looked around for Eddie. It wasn't the sight of her guide flirting with the clerk, that caught her attention, however. It was the man standing a couple hundred feet past him.

The ground seemed to rock beneath her feet. She closed her eyes, reopened them, expecting to discover that the man was a stranger, like the rest of the people in the crowd. But he wasn't. He was the man in the composite the police artist had done. The completed sketch of the person who had shot at her, days before.

Without conscious thought she moved closer to Eddie's side, blocking the man's view of her. He was four or five booths down, on the same side of the street. She peered around Eddie's form, waiting to get a better look at him.

After several seconds he faced the vendor, holding up two hatbands and talking rapidly. While the clerk brought out another tray of wares to show him, the man glanced around, giving Delaney a full view of his face.

Her last shred of doubt was dashed. This was the man who'd wielded the rifle. She shifted again, before he could catch sight of her. "Here you go." Eddie turned and handed her a piece of corn cake. "Best taste and the best price. You'll thank me later."

"I'll thank you now if you'll do something for me." She gave him a nudge to get him to move a few inches away. "Look to your right at the man picking out hatbands." She sighed as he looked past her. "No, your other right. There. See him? Black hat? Red-and-black shirt?"

"The guy buying the concha shell band? He's getting ripped off. Sheballa does the best workmanship, but I don't see him here today. He's usually set up at the end of this row."

"Eddie," she whispered urgently, "Concentrate! I want you to take my camera. Saunter closer, casually," she stressed, "and act like you're taking pictures of the vendors and the wares. Make sure you've got him in every picture you take, but don't *act* like you're taking his picture. Got it?"

"Not really."

She took the corn cake and tripod from him and shoved the camera in his hand, showed him how to focus and snap the shot. "Quickly. Before he leaves." Giving him a little push, she faded behind a trio that stepped up for an order of fry bread and Eddie looked around, seeming a little lost.

In a moment, however he raised the camera and ambled away. Delaney let out a breath of relief. Her plans for the rest of the day abruptly morphed. She wanted to get these pictures to Joe, to see if he agreed that the man was the one they were looking for. She moved to keep Eddie and the man in sight, while still keeping people between them.

The stranger was leaving. Eddie continued to snap pictures, as she walked up behind him. "Let's see what you got."

The guide looked at her oddly, but handed over the

camera and took a piece of the corn cake she held. "Okay, do you want to tell me why a guy buying a hatband is so important for your book? Because if you've got a thing for hats, I've got a half dozen of them at home, all with better-looking bands than the one that guy bought."

"Sorry." She set down the tripod and viewed the pictures he'd taken, surprised at the number he'd managed with clear shots. "Nice job. Maybe I could make a photographer of you." Then she happened across one plainly focused on the bosom of the girl they'd passed earlier on the way to the market. "Or maybe not."

"I said I was flexible," he reminded her, his mouth full of corn cake. "Never said I was blind. Or stupid. What the heck is going on?"

She started strolling in the same direction as the man they'd photographed, heading away from the flea market. "I think I know that man from somewhere."

"So instead of going up to talk to him, you take secret pictures of him." He took another bite, swallowed.

"Well, he sort of tried to kill me a few days ago so I'm not feeling especially friendly. C'mon." She hastened her stride, keeping her head down. "I want to follow him."

But Eddie had stopped in his tracks. "He tried to kill you? Why?"

With an impatient gesture she hurried him along. "I don't know. Maybe he doesn't like photographers.

Maybe he prefers blondes. Whatever his motive, I'd like to find out, wouldn't you?" There was no use telling him what she knew about the man's motives, which was depressingly little. "The police are looking for him and I want them to find him, so let's go."

They trailed him for a block or so, lagging well behind, but keeping him in sight. When he got into a pickup Delaney attached the zoom lens to her camera. She stepped into the street, brought the camera up again and took several pictures as he was driving away.

Eddie watched her, clearly at a loss for words. "Well, now what? You still want to go to Monument Valley?"

"Maybe later." She lowered the camera, staring after the truck pensively. "First I need to go to the police."

"You're getting to be a popular guy, Joe." Vicki Smith didn't bother to try and hide the curiosity in her gaze when she showed Delaney and a strange man to the computer he was logging off of.

He rose, looking from Delaney to the man he assumed was the guide the council had hired for her. "I thought you were going to Monument Valley today."

"We were. But first we went to the flea market. You're not going to believe this. Look." She held the LCD screen of her camera up to him and began flipping through the pictures Eddie had taken.

He looked obediently, his brows rising when he saw one in particular. "I'm not sure that young lady would appreciate your interest in her cleavage."

Her sigh was exasperated. "Men. Look at the guy in the hat. Does he seem familiar to you? At all?"

Joe looked closer, and recognition flickered. "Maybe. Let's get these on the computer screen for a comparison."

He shot a look at the man standing silently behind them. "And you are?"

"That's Eddie Bahe. My guide. Eddie, special investigator Joe Youngblood."

Bahe, who had looked more than a little uncomfortable since he'd come in, looked distinctly more so as Joe continued to stare at him. He smiled weakly. "I'm going to be helping the lady out while she's on the Rez."

"Don't tell me. That was your handiwork we saw on the camera."

He gave a halfhearted shrug. "Never claimed to be a photographer."

Joe figured that he could guess exactly what Bahe *did* claim to be, but Delaney's voice interrupted his thoughts. "Did a match show up for the composite?"

"No. Which just means the guy had no prior convictions. Or that the composite sketch wasn't accurate enough."

Soon Delaney was seated in the chair before the computer, Joe and Eddie hanging over her shoulder, peering at the pictures and comparing them to the likeness on the sketch. Joe reached forward to tap the screen. "Let's see that one again." When Delaney zoomed in on the full frontal view of the man, he and

Eddie leaned forward simultaneously for a better look, their shoulders butting.

Joe shot the other man a narrowed look and Eddie backed up, smiling sheepishly. "Sorry."

For several long moments, Joe looked from the picture to the composite. "No way to be sure," he muttered, "given the way we put that sketch together. But it seems close. Real close."

"That's what I thought." Delaney selected another photo. "So now you can go talk to him."

"I'll be glad to do that, once I…" He stopped as a picture appeared on the screen of an older model blue pickup driving away. She zoomed in on the license plate. "Quite the little detective, aren't you?" He went to his desk, got a piece of paper and a pen and came back to scribble down the number. "I'll run this through the MVD. Bring up the other shots of the truck, will you?"

As she obeyed Eddie spoke up. "1992, '93 blue Dodge Ram. Original wheels, missing a hubcap on the left back driver's side. Dented tailgate."

Joe looked over his shoulder and Eddie shrugged. "I said photography wasn't my thing. Cars and trucks are."

"Okay. Leave the pictures on the screen. I'll check it out."

Delaney didn't move from the chair. "If you want me to, I could…"

"What I want," he said, making an attempt to gentle his voice, "is for you to continue doing whatever it is you and Bahe had planned." With one hand on her arm, he guided her to a standing position. "Take all the pictures you want. But don't go chasing down people who have used you for target practice. I'll take it from here."

She faced him, her expression mutinous. "But thanks a lot, Delaney, for just making my job a whole lot easier."

Something in him lightened at the reminder of their earlier conversation and he had an urge to cup that angled jaw and kiss that sarcastic mouth. The inclination was totally out of character for him. His involvement with her at all was totally out of character, which should have scared the hell out of him.

"Nice job. Now I'll take it from here." It was almost worth it to see her eyes go stormy, the band of gold widening around the iris. He could see what her shrug cost her, as she picked up her camera and packed it away in its case again.

"Keep me posted."

His voice was mild. "I'll do that."

He watched her walk out of the room, until he saw Officer Garcia smirking. "You finished typing up your report on that list of Quintero's clients?"

"On your desk. Nothing stood out to me, but maybe something will jump for you. I did get a couple of them to admit they'd seen Mary Barlow around when they'd 'talked' to Quintero."

He grunted. So the woman had lied to him about that, not that he was surprised. Faced with a cop, it was most people's first instinct. Maybe it was time to talk to her again.

Checking Tapahe's window, it appeared the man was

off the phone. Joe headed for the door. First he wanted to get permission to set up some surveillance on Graywolf and see if they could find a stronger connection between him and Quintero. He was willing to spend as long as it took to convince Tapahe that they had enough to do so. And then he'd run the plates on the man who might just turn out to be Delaney's shooter. Tracking him down would give Joe every bit as much satisfaction as nailing Graywolf.

"So explain this to me again," Abra Garcia said. "The guy we're going to talk to was driving a stolen truck?"

"It hasn't been reported as stolen." Joe slowed to a stop in front of the address he'd been seeking. The blue truck was sitting in the dirt drive. "But it's not listed under his name."

"So this isn't necessarily his place?" Abra Garcia looked at the small dingy white house, with the screens and outside door missing.

"We're about to find out."

They got out of his unmarked police issue Jeep and headed up to the front door. Joe knocked and they waited. He tried again, more loudly this time, and finally the front door opened a crack, and a middle-aged woman peered out at them.

"*¿Quiénes son usted?*"

"Sergeant Joe Youngblood, ma'am. Criminal Investigations." Joe showed his shield and continued, "This is Navajo Tribal Police Officer Garcia. Is that your truck in the drive?"

"*Si.*" She switched to English. "It is my husband's truck."

"May we speak to him?"

Her eyes were rounded, plainly worried. "He works. He is not here now. What is the worry?"

"There's no trouble, ma'am." Garcia put in smoothly. "We had a report that the person driving this truck a couple hours ago may have witnessed an accident downtown and we're just following up on that. Were you driving?"

She shook her head slowly. "I do not drive in this country. My son, Niyol."

Joe took over. "Your son was driving? Is he here? It would be very helpful if we could speak to him."

Her expression eased slightly. "*Un momento.*" The door shut again and they waited for several minutes before the woman came back to open the door, biting her lip. "Niyol was here, but now he is gone. I did not see him leave."

Exchanging a glance with Garcia, Joe said, "How long ago did you see him, Mrs...?"

"Lee. Maria Lee. Niyol was here five minutes before. Five minutes." She nodded her head emphatically.

Meaning he headed out the back door the second he saw them pulling up to the house, Joe thought cynically. "Do you mind if we look out back? See if he's still around?"

After a moment's hesitation the woman shook her head and Joe lost no time rounding the house, only to find the backyard deserted. There was no sign of life in the yards of the nearby houses, either. Rejoining

Garcia on the front porch, he asked, "Do you know when he'll be back? Does he live here with you and your husband?"

"He stays with us sometimes. He lives in Mexico and sometimes he lives here. He was born in Mexico City but his father is Navajo. He has…" She searched for the correct phrase.

"Dual citizenship?"

"*Si.*"

"Do you mind if we come inside? Look around?"

The woman looked from one to the other of them and then stepped back, allowing them entry into the house.

It was as suffocating as an oven. Almost immediately Joe could feel perspiration dampen his face. He looked through the house. It was sparsely furnished, but there was a telephone, a newer model television and running water.

"What a pretty wall hanging," he heard Garcia say in back of him. "Did you make it?"

He took advantage of their distraction to peer into a cramped bedroom on his left. There was a large crucifix hanging over the bed, a woman's clothing interspersed with a man's in the cramped open closet. The parents' bedroom.

The door across the hallway was shut. Joe turned the knob, and stepped to the side as the door swung open. But it was as empty as the other rooms appeared to be. An open window indicated the man's probable exit.

Swiftly he checked the closet, looked under the bed and mattress, went through the dresser drawers, not sure exactly what he was looking for. He found it, though, taped to the back of the dresser. A small notebook and a bankbook.

The women's voices were coming closer. He tore the items free of the tape and flipped through them. A savings account at a Flagstaff bank showed that Niyol Lee had deposited sums of five thousand dollars almost monthly for the last three years. Dropping the bankbook on the bed, he opened the notebook, which seemed to be a combination of jotted initials and dates. It was the first of the initials that caught Joe's eye, though. B.G.

He resecured both books behind the dresser a second before the two women appeared in the doorway, but his mind continued to race. B.G.

Brant Graywolf?

"I don't understand the connection."

It had been late when Joe appeared on Delaney's step, but she hadn't been asleep. She suspected he knew that; that he understood sleep didn't come easily to her. And she appreciated the fact that he didn't comment on it.

"I don't know the connection yet," Joe admitted. He picked up his plate and took it to the sink, rinsing it off, and the hominess of the gesture almost succeeded in distracting her. She'd made him eggs, one of the few meals she could manage without burning and he'd eaten with a single-minded intensity that told her better than words how long it had been since he'd last eaten.

He turned to face her, leaning back against the counter. "But Graywolf is linked to Quintero. Quintero might be linked to those three kids who were murdered three weeks ago." She shuddered, remembering the short succinct description he'd given her of the scene. "And Lee is linked to you, because we're pretty sure he's the one who fired those shots a few days ago. Now it's looking like he might also be linked to Graywolf."

"You can't be sure those initials are his."

"No," Joe admitted. "But all initials and dates in that book seemed to correlate to the dates of the deposits made in Lee's bank account." He unbuckled his holster, wrapped the straps around the sheathed weapon. "Lee's mother said he only stayed there some of the time when he was in the area, so maybe he's got another place to hide. But something tells me the three of them—the guy shooting at you, Graywolf and Quintero—are all connected."

"Why would someone keep records that could incriminate them?" She trailed after him as he left the kitchen and walked into her bedroom, where he set the gun on the dresser. He sat on the edge of the bed, and starting pulling off his boots.

Delaney's stomach jittered oddly at the sight. He shrank the space when he was in it. Heck, he stamped the whole house with his presence. And it all seemed too much, too soon. The familiarity of his showing up here. Her feeding him. Even talking about the case. It all seemed so...*domestic*.

The term had her mouth drying out. She didn't do domestic and she certainly didn't do long-term. Just the thought had anxiety skating along her nerves. She was used to being the outsider, always looking in, always observing. There was a certain distance necessary to see all angles of the story.

It had never bothered her before, it was just something that *was,* like her hair or eye color. It wasn't until she'd finished her last project and allowed herself to go home, her nerves in shreds, nightmares and alcohol sharing a viselike grip on her psyche, that she realized the truth—she didn't *belong* anywhere anymore. She could go home but she couldn't be *at* home there. And the sincere love and support her family had tried to offer had, at times, felt as smothering as the flashbacks that dragged her back into the past.

She wasn't sure why that fact struck her now, except that she'd never seen a man with a stronger sense of belonging than Joe Youngblood. His ties to his culture, to his family were so much a part of him that one couldn't be separated from the other. And knowing that filled her with a sort of wistfulness, as if he had something she didn't want. Didn't need. But recognized all the same as something she'd never have.

He was staring at her and she realized with a start that he'd been speaking. "I'm sorry, what?"

"I said Lee might be keeping it to incriminate someone else. It might be insurance in case he gets caught at whatever the hell he's doing, so he has something to trade." His T-shirt came off next and the sight of that wide expanse of hard bronzed flesh had all doubts and distractions receding. She looked away, the blood in her pulse turning slow and heavy.

The silence in the room went thick.

"Delaney."

She swallowed, struggled to tuck away the unfamiliar tide of emotion that threatened to flood her. It was so much easier not to feel at all, to avoid feelings that brought pain more often than anything else. How had she forgotten that? And why?

Slowly, she met his gaze.

"I can go."

It'd be better if he did. Better if they both had time to recall all the reasons this was to be kept casual. Emotionless.

But the thought of sending him out that door, alone, didn't leave her feeling casual or emotionless. Whatever the cost, she realized, she'd made her choice the first night she'd slept with him. All she could do was hope that the cost wouldn't be too great. "I want you to stay."

His dark gaze searched hers, but when she went to him, smoothed her hands over the bunched muscles in his shoulders, the tension seemed to seep away.

He pulled her closer, spread one large palm on her bottom while his other hand slipped under her shirt. "You sure?"

Already desire was trumping doubt. A thousand tiny flames flickered to life beneath the skin where he touched her. She pressed her lips against his and whispered, "No. But I'm willing to be convinced."

Chapter 10

"I told you before, I'm done talking to you." Mary Barlow raised her chin mutinously, but her gaze kept darting beyond Joe to the street in front of her motel.

"And I told you I know you were lying about not being aware of Oree's activities. You were there when many of his drug transactions went down. I've got people who will testify to that. Makes you an accessory, Mary. I can charge you with that."

She licked her lips, and for a moment he almost felt sorry for her. The days since he'd last seen her had not been kind to the woman. She looked as if she hadn't slept, and it was obvious someone had used her for a punching bag. Her lip was split and there was a multicolored bruise beneath one eye.

"Do what you gotta do." Her attempt at bravado fell flat. "I don't believe you can get anyone to testify. They're all just as scared as I am."

Interest piqued he leaned forward. "Who are they afraid of, Mary? The same person who did that to your face?"

"I ran into a door," she muttered.

"Must have had a fist attached to it. You could file a report, you know. Whoever did that could be brought in and charged."

She made a derisive sound. "As if you guys could get anything to stick to him. His daddy's money would have him on the street in an hour and an hour after *that* I'd be dead."

Stunned, Joe just stared at her for a moment. "Are you saying Graywolf did that to you?"

"I'm done talking. Didn't have anything to say to you last time, but that didn't stop me from getting this." She fingered the bruise beneath her eye.

Adrenaline spiked through him. "If you've got information about Brant Graywolf we can protect you. If you just tell me what you know, I can make sure…"

"No one can be protected from Brant." A car driving by seemed to spook her, and she bolted by him, heading for her vehicle. "If you don't believe me, ask those three kids they found a few weeks back." She yanked open her door but before she got inside she sent him a bitter smile. "Oh, that's right. You can't. They're dead."

* * *

"They're waiting for you in the captain's office."

Joe looked from Vicki Smith to the area she indicated, but the blinds covering the office window were closed. "Any idea what's going on?"

Vicki shook her head, the action sending her brunette bob swaying. "All I know is someone from Border Patrol walked in asking for you, and five minutes later Captain was telling me to get on the radio, and get you in here."

Border Patrol? Joe immediately thought of Bernie Silversmith, and his step quickened. Maybe he'd discovered something about the tread he'd faxed him.

But the man with Tapahe wasn't Bernie Silversmith. He was a white man, short, balding and stocky, with a permanently rosy complexion. Ruddy skin met pale in a horizontal dissection across his broad forehead, where constant hat-wearing had protected his scalp.

"Joe." Tapahe greeted him. "This is Border Patrol Supervisor Clint Dawson." Dawson rose. He had a white man's handshake, firm, held a trifle too long, as opposed to the Navajo preferred manner of only a light touching of the hands. "I spoke to Bernie Silversmith about you. He says you're a good cop."

Joe lifted a shoulder. "He has to say that. He still owes me money from the last time we played poker."

Dawson smiled briefly. "I'll remind him of that the next time I see him." He reseated himself. "Bernie posted that tread you'd faxed him on an interagency Web bulletin board and it drew some immediate interest. I was just telling your captain here that we've run across that same tread a couple dozen times in the last few years."

"Have you matched it to a make and model?"

The man's blue eyes glinted. "We've done better than that. We've gotten a description of the vehicle it belongs to. A 1998 Econoline four-wheel drive van that's been seen in the vicinity of known crossing points. The coyote smuggles the illegals across the border on foot, the van picks them up and they vanish."

Joe digested the bit of news. "Coyotes," or guides who took money from people wishing to enter the United States illegally, were known for their ruthless cunning. With nearly two thousand miles of southern border for the Border Patrol to protect, they were too often successful at finding ways to get their clients across. It wasn't uncommon to hear of the guides taking the money and then beating or killing their customers. "When you say they vanish…"

Dawson looked grim. "I mean their families never hear from them again. We haven't found any bodies. They just disappear. The Mexican government has looked into it, but they haven't found any unidentified remains, either."

"A coyote wouldn't take them over the border, just to kill illegals here," Joe interjected. "So what does that leave? Slavery?" It was one thing for the criminals to take a few thousand dollars for sneaking people into the country. It was quite another to bring them in and then hand them over to human traffickers to be exploited in the sex trade, farm fields or as household labor.

"Possibly. And there have always been coyotes offering reduced fees for clients willing to act as mules. But in the last year we've been hearing of one getting the illegals to carry loads of a purified form of crystal ice purchased from a cartel down there. And the last time we saw that tread, we found traces of ice at the crossing nearby." Dawson shrugged. "Right now that's all we've got."

Excitement rose, simmered. This was the connection, finally, to Quintero, Graywolf and Lee. Joe could feel it. He remembered the bottled water, blankets and food wrappers that had littered the cave. Exactly what would be needed to hide a bunch of illegals until the next stage of their journeys. "Maybe it's time to flag that syringe as a priority," he said to the captain. He was willing to bet that they'd find traces of Rohypnol or some other tranquilizer used to render the aliens helpless before transporting them to their captors.

"You read my mind," Tapahe replied. "I'll call the lab. You contact the other members of the task force and see how quickly you can get them here."

The table around the conference room was crowded, despite it being a Sunday evening. John Honani, the Hopi DEA agent, sat silently amidst the buzz in the room. FBI agent Delmer Mitchell was trying, unsuccessfully, to add creamer to his coffee without it splashing on his stained suit. Dawson was back, along with Manny Lopez, a Customs Service supervisor coordinating that agency's cooperating officers. Quentin Tarken was another fed, apparently working with Mitchell. Joe had never met him before.

Because he knew Arnie would never let him hear the end of it, Joe had called him, and the man had been only too eager to leave the overly solicitous care of his wife. When everyone was finally seated, Joe said, "I think the easiest way to bring everyone up to date is to let individuals discuss their part of the case. Then we'll talk about the newest developments." He turned to Honani. "John, do you want to begin?"

"We've had an informant in the Contreres cartel feeding us information on their expansions of super-labs," the man began. "They took advantage of the States' new controls on ingredients for homemade meth by cranking up the production of the purer, more lethal crystal ice we've seen flooding the country. Joe and Arnie were investigating an influx of the drug here, and because we had reason to believe some of the Contreres supply was ending up in these parts, we decided to coordinate our efforts."

Joe's mind drifted as each task member briefly relayed their role in the investigation and information on the case. Surveillance on Graywolf hadn't yielded a thing so far, and Joe was beginning to question whether he was attributing the kid with too large a part in this deal. They could ill-afford to waste resources. It took a lot of manpower to watch him round the clock, with officers on foot and in cars. So far they'd estab-lished his routine of going to work in the headquarters of his father's construction firm somewhere close to noon, and leaving again around five. Nice hours if one could get them. From there he visited with friends, all of whom were being checked out, or went back to the family home, located on one of the largest privately owned pieces of property on Navajo Nation lands.

The Graywolfs enjoyed a standard of living unrivaled on the reservation, which probably accounted for the kid's spoiled manner. Riches in their culture weren't traditionally attributed to money or material goods but measured in family and connection to their past. That had been one of Charley's teachings that Joe had taken to heart, much to Heather's dismay. Toward the end of their marriage all she'd talked about was the promise of better opportunities off the reservation.

His attention snapped back to the conversation at hand, as Dawson was winding down. Joe gave a succinct description of his efforts and the events in the last several days, ending with the notebook pages he'd perused in Niyol Lee's bedroom.

There was a moment of silence as the members digested the information. "And the last date in his book…when was that again?"

"Two days from now," Joe answered. "The other dates seemed to be correlated within a day or two of a deposit in his savings account. It's not a stretch to believe that Lee is getting paid well for providing a service, and he has dual citizenship, allowing him to move freely between here and Mexico."

Rising, he passed out copies of the composite sketch of the man.

"If your witness can make a positive ID of Lee as the guy who shot at her, we've got enough to go in and search Lee's parents' home. Seize the bankbook, notebook and anything you might have missed." Tarken rubbed his jaw, dark with five o'clock shadow.

"Maria Lee would probably give it to us without one," Joe said, ignoring the obvious slur on his abilities. "But why tip off Niyol more than we already have? Right now he doesn't realize we know something is going down, so there's no reason for them to change their plans. It seems more productive for us to figure out where it's going to happen, or at least where they'll be bringing the illegals so we can nail them then."

"There are thousands of places on the reservation that would hide a vanload of aliens and several hundred kilos of meth." This from Manny. "With the slot canyons, cliff dwellings and caves in the area, we could search for months trying to find where they moved their operation."

"I think we can rule out any public area," Arnie put in. "Too risky. The area has to be remote, yet vehicles have to be able to get in and out. Somewhat close to a road, because a van, even four-wheel drive, isn't going to do cross-country for long stretches."

Joe glanced at the man approvingly. Even with his absence in the last few days, they remained on the same wavelength. "Exactly. Last time they had it all planned out. Accessed an isolated spot where they could have some privacy. A perfect system, actually, because they made sure they weren't going to get sheepherders wandering through there with their flocks, either. It's too soon for them to have arranged another place like that, so they had to move quickly, maybe to an area not so perfect."

"Or they may just cancel this run until they find someplace perfect."

Joe looked at Tarken curiously. He seemed more truculent than helpful, and Mitchell, in his presence, didn't speak up much. "You're forgetting the guy we saw leaving on the ATV. He had it piled with parcels, which makes sense if the van was full of people. They were moving shop not cutting and running."

Delmer Mitchell finally spoke up. "I thought I read about lots of abandoned mines on these lands. What about one of them?"

"Most are on public lands," Joe said slowly, considering the idea. "And a lot were sealed off in recent years, when government funding was used for the reclamation act."

"But not all of them," Arnie mused. "And I think they focused on the abandoned uranium mines, because they presented the biggest risk. It's worth checking into."

"I still say it's a needle in a haystack," Tarken said flatly. "We can't waste federal resources putting together a sting on a possible coyote run unless we have better intelligence than this." There was agreement in the expressions of the other federal agents, with the exception of Honani, who remained impassive. "Get us something more concrete. All of us should go back to pulling on the threads we've been working. Maybe something will shake loose."

As if his remark had signaled an end to the meeting, the men began to push away from the table and stand. Dawson came over as the agents were filing out of the room. "Lopez and I can at least put out bulletins for officers to watch for that van on the date you mentioned. It's a long shot, but someone might spot it. And we can show copies of that composite around, too."

Joe thanked him politely and the Border Patrol agent followed the others out the door. But the man had been right. It was a long shot, and from all accounts, Lee, if he was the driver of the van, had a long and successful career outwitting the officers dotting the States' southern border.

"So what now?" Arnie asked when the room was once again empty. "I still think that mine idea has merit. Maybe we should focus on that."

"With only two days to work with, we need to narrow the search. A place close to here," Joe murmured, his mind racing. "A place that might not be a permanent site, but where they have reason to believe they'd be safe."

"A mine that hasn't been reclaimed in a really remote part of the reservation," Arnie said doggedly. "Say, within a seventy-mile radius of the last spot."

"Or a place where few people could travel freely," Joe mused. "Like private property."

The other man got up and went to the coffeemaker, picked up the carafe and shook the miniscule remaining amount in disgust. "They wouldn't have time to arrange another lease so quickly." He replaced the container on the coffeemaker and came back to the table.

"But what if one of them had property they could use? Just until something else gets obtained." A glimmer of an idea was taking hold. "Who has access to more property than a third of the tribe combined?"

"Graywolf?" Arnie sank into a chair. "Well, his family has property. And the construction company would have a lot of sites that could be possible areas, too."

Joe shook his head. "Too much traffic in and out of a construction site. No, if it were me, I'd pick a place I knew. One I could be pretty sure would be left alone. And even better if I knew no one could get to it without trespassing."

"The kid would be taking a heck of a risk."

The more Joe considered the idea, the more it made sense. "He thinks he's smarter than we are. He thinks he's above the law. He got caught several times for dealing, with barely a slap on the wrist. A track record like that might convince the kid he's infallible, instead of realizing he owes it all to smooth lawyers and family money."

"Maybe he's not calling the shots at all, maybe his father is—did you ever think of that?"

"There's nothing pointing that way, but if he were, it would be one more reason to focus on Graywolf land for the new site." Joe got up and strode to his desk where he'd stacked the information they'd gotten from the land office, took out a map of the Navajo lands and spread it across his desk.

"And you said my desk is bad," Arnie commented,

trailing out to watch Joe quizzically. "Looks like you became a slob in my absence. What is all this?"

"Information." Joe grabbed a section of maps and property documentation and thrust it toward his partner. "I needed to find out who owned that piece of land where Delaney was shot at, and Garcia brought a whole box of this stuff back from the land office. Start going through it. Maybe we can find something on the Graywolf holdings."

Although he wasn't looking up, he could hear the smirk in his friend's voice. "Delaney? Would that be the lady you didn't want on the reservation?"

Deliberately, Joe kept his gaze trained on the map. "Like you said, Charley and I had different opinions. It really doesn't have anything to do with Carson."

"Oh, really." Arnie went to his desk with his pile of papers and sat down. "Seems to me that the case isn't the only thing I need to be caught up on."

But Joe wasn't about to say anything further. Whatever this thing was between him and Delaney, it wasn't something he wanted to share. It wasn't even something he could easily identify to himself.

It'd be easy to tell himself that sex was all that bound them. Easy to accept the boundaries she'd so carefully laid out for their relationship. But it was hard to reconcile a casual no-strings liaison with the need that was beginning to burn in him at the oddest times when she wasn't near. Or with the sense of contentment he felt with her curled up beside him, as she slipped uneasily into a troubled sleep.

It was dangerous for a man to allow a woman close enough to fill parts of himself he hadn't realized were empty. And it was far more dangerous to let such a woman know that she wielded that kind of power. He had no intention of doing either. He knew Delaney Carson well enough to be certain that would frighten her at least as much as it did him.

The sunsets on the land of *Dinetah* would always remain the most spectacular in her memory. Delaney finally lowered her camera and sat down on the ground in back of her small house to enjoy the final display of crimson bleeding over the horizon. Her computer was already loaded with similar images, far more than she needed for the book. But the rest were for her. Brilliant washes of color to remind her of the Navajo custom of finding beauty all around them.

Saturday had been spent with Eddie in her first visit to Monument Valley. She'd quickly discovered how naive it had been to assume she could "see" a place so vast in one day, so they'd focused on the southern end, around Hunt's Mesa. It had taken her four-wheel drive and some hiking to get them to the more inaccessible parts, but the landscape of lonely buttes and sculpted red rock formations had taken her breath away.

There had been a sort of sacredness about the place that quieted the spirit and hushed the soul. One that hinted of centuries-old ghosts and long-dead secrets. She'd been left with a lingering sense of sadness that she'd never truly understand what it meant to the *Diné* to stand in that place. And a sort of peace that came from being there at all.

Although she didn't hear his approach, she felt a presence behind her and knew instinctively who it was. "You missed it," she murmured. Shadows were spreading along the darkened horizon and the sky had grayed. "Do you ever get used to that kind of beauty day after day?"

He'd squatted down behind her. She could feel his breath in her hair and had the urge to lean against him, to feel his strength and warmth envelop her. She squelched the temptation. A woman who got too used to leaning on someone else could easily forget how to rely solely on herself.

"Grandfather would say that when a man stops seeing the beauty around him, he also stops seeing himself and his place in the world."

"And what would Joe Youngblood say?" She didn't know where this compulsion sprang from, to scratch below the surface for glimpses of the enigmatic man beneath.

"No," he said simply. "I never get used to it."

She would have been content to sit and watch the stars break through the night sky as it darkened but she sensed a restlessness in the man behind her. Rising, she dusted off her jeans as they headed to the house.

"I spent a day with Cowboy Nahkai," she informed him as they entered the living room. The hours she'd spent with the older man had been an intriguing glimpse into a mystical part of the culture. The crystal gazer had explained his role as a diagnostician of various ailments, and the resulting recommendation for the proper ceremonies or chants to focus on healing.

"When people like Cowboy and other medicine people die, too often their knowledge dies with them. Already there are fewer ceremonies done than when I was a boy. Fewer chants remain well-known."

"They need to be documented," she said, horrified at the thought of traditions being lost forever.

"Applying for the job?" But where the words would have been caustic when they first met, she detected a note of teasing in them now.

"No. Even I can agree that it would be a job best done by a tribe member for the tribe."

He sank heavily onto the sofa and for the first time she noted the fatigue on his face. It was evident that he'd been keeping long hours, and not for the reason she did, pushing herself to work until well after midnight hoping to drop into the bone-weary sleep of the exhausted.

"Are you hungry? I have…" She took mental inventory of her cupboards. "Peanut butter."

"Tempting. But, no. I stopped at Charley's before coming here." He reached up for her hand and gave it a tug, so she sat on the arm of the sofa next to him. It didn't escape her notice that he didn't relinquish his hold on her, but laced their fingers together. "He rarely loses an opportunity to feed me, or to nag about proper nutrition."

"He worries about you," she murmured. He rested his head against the back of the couch and closed his eyes. She was tempted to smooth the lines from his face. Her free hand rose, hovered, before dropping into her lap again. She moistened her lips. "I can see it in his expression when he talks about your job. He's proud of you, but he's worried, too. He said…" She thought back, trying to recall the phrase correctly. "…that coyote is always out there waiting and coyote is always hungry."

Coyote was a recurring figure in Navajo lore, appearing in most native legends, portrayed both as an essential figure that gave order to life, and an association with evil. If Charley had been referring to the dangers inherent in Joe's job, she could certainly understand the reference.

He made a sound of agreement, although he didn't open his eyes. "We have another saying, too. 'It's impossible to wake a man who is pretending to be asleep.' I'm careful. I have to be. Charley knows that, but he'll worry anyway." He gave a fatalistic shrug.

He tugged on her hand, hard enough to have her tumbling into his arms and his eyes opened then, a satisfied glint in them. "The case might be coming to a head."

It was difficult to concentrate on his words when she was all too aware of her unfamiliar position. She'd never been a lap-sitter. She doubted she'd sat on a man's lap since she'd perched on her dad's as a child. But as one of his arms came around her to pull her closer, a bit of the stiffness left her limbs and she leaned a little against him, letting herself enjoy his nearness.

He was still talking. "Arnie and I discovered that there's an abandoned coal mine on the Graywolf property."

"They own a coal mine?"

"It was started several years prior to the Black Mesa mining agreement and probably closed when a big operation was built."

"So what's an old coal mine have to do with your drug case?"

"Not just the drug case, as it turns out." She listened, with growing amazement, as he explained how the events at the cave site overlapped with the case he was investigating. "If that date in a couple days means another run to the border, they need a place that is relatively safe and out of sight."

Her throat went thick at the mere thought of forcing the aliens into a dark, yawning shaft, leaving them to wait in vain for what they incorrectly thought would be their bid for a better life.

"So if you know where the mine is, you can catch them red-handed."

"Not exactly." His voice was dry. "The mine is only a possibility at this point, certainly not enough to get us a warrant. We have to figure a way to narrow down the possibilities and get some hard evidence. A judge isn't going to let us on private property with only supposition."

She hadn't considered that. They couldn't check it out without more evidence to connect Graywolf to the investigation.

And they had only two days to find it.

A thought circled, barely formed. "Do you suspect the Graywolf family is involved, or just the son?" She felt his hand loosening the knot of her hair, allowing it to tumble around her shoulders.

"There's nothing to point to Graywolf senior, and I'd be surprised if he were in on this thing."

It was on the tip of her tongue to mention her idea, but after a second she thought better of it. She knew what Joe's response would be, and it was always easier to ask forgiveness than permission. At any rate, he was exhausted and needed sleep.

She remained silent while he rose, with her in his arms, and walked to her bedroom. She stripped to camisole and panties and joined him in bed. His arm snaked out to pull her close, one of his legs covering both of hers, but he seemed content just to have her close, her cheek pressed to his chest.

And something suspiciously like contentment traced through her, as she felt her body relax and follow him into a deep and dreamless slumber.

She was suffocating. Facedown in rubble that used to be walls, floors, ceilings. Pinned beneath a giant invisible weight, every breath an agony.

The screams and moans of the dying were constant companions, slashing at her eardrums, echoing her anguish. But worse, far worse was when the screaming finally stopped. When she became aware that she was the only one left, buried alive in this crushing prison to die alone. One torturous moment at a time.

She struggled against that frantic certainty. Battled wildly against the constant pressure that held her immobile. Knowing all the while that she'd join the silent ghosts all around her....

"Delaney. Wake up."

It wasn't the soft command that had her eyes snapping open. It was the sudden release of the pressure that held her pinned. Support beams from the ceiling, maybe. Or stones from the pillars that had once dotted the hotel lobby.

She blinked, comprehension returning sluggishly. The dust that had filled her lungs only moments ago was gone. She was in a darkened room but the corpses around her had vanished. There was only a man, his expression grim and worried, surveying her carefully.

Understanding rushed in, mingled with humiliation. "I'm sorry."

"Don't apologize." The words were sharp, though his tone was low. "Are you all right?"

She let out a laugh, one bitter breath, and scrambled off the bed. It was a wreck, sheets tangled, trailing on the floor from her fight to free herself of the nightmare's grasp. And Joe's. Her gaze bounced to him again. "Did I hurt you?"

The oath he uttered was dangerous. "Forget that. Are you all right?"

"I'm fine." But she stumbled away from the bed, unwilling, unable to face it again. "I'll be fine. Try to get some sleep."

He followed her out into the other room, having

pulled on his jeans without bothering to fasten them. She could feel him watching her in the shadows, and wished bitterly that she could prevent the shudders racking her body. Stop the nausea clenching and roiling in her stomach. And felt that familiar helpless fury when her body didn't obey her mind and the shivers continued to skate over her sweat-slicked skin.

"Maybe you should go." The walls of the room seemed to be pressing in. She was suddenly anxious to have him gone, before she disgraced herself completely and bolted from the house like a demented mental patient. "You aren't going to get any sleep here, and you need it."

He didn't answer, but went back to the bedroom. She let out a pent-up breath and forced herself to walk, not race, to the front door. She fumbled with the lock and yanked it open, stumbling out onto the porch to haul in a greedy gulp of air, feeling marginally more normal just to be outside.

Normal. An ironic little smile settled on her lips. What passed for normal these days was a far cry from most people's definition of the word. It took effort to remember what it had been like before she feared sleep. Before just the thought of enclosed places had her palms dampening, her pulse racing. When she had a little distance to recover from this latest episode she'd remind herself that the nightmares occurred less frequently. That she was, for all intents, moving ahead with her life despite all that had come before.

But now, in the dark and desperate hours of the night, the reassurances were empty.

"Come with me."

Joe had appeared behind her, and she didn't miss the care he took not to touch her. "No, I'll see you later. Maybe when this thing is all over."

He did reach out then, laying his palm on her shoulder to caress her arm in a long velvet stroke. "Let me show you something." Reluctantly she followed him back into the house, both surprised and relieved when he headed through it, then out the back doorway and down the steps.

The quarter moon was smudged by inky fingers of dark clouds, but the stars were bright overhead, brilliant pinpricks of light glimmering against the black velvet sky. Feeling a little lost, she stumbled after him, her feet not nearly as sure as his in the darkness.

"Here."

He'd made a bed of sorts from what looked like the sofa and chair cushions and her bedding. The thoughtfulness of the gesture stung her eyelids.

"I spent more time sleeping outside than in during months like this when I was a kid. It still brings me peace when something is troubling me." He sank down on the pallet and pulled at her hand so that she landed beside him. With swift economical movements he got her situated next to him and pulled a sheet over them both.

"Peace can be elusive," she murmured. But something resembling it settled in her now, with her head tucked beneath Joe's shoulder, his arm around her and a billion tiny shards of light twinkling above her.

Though he was silent for a long time, she knew he

wasn't sleeping. His voice, when he finally spoke, was halting. "Does it bother you to talk about it? Make it worse?"

"Not really." She stared unblinkingly at the constellations above. And that was true. Talking changed nothing. She'd become convinced that only time accomplished that, but had never imagined how excruciatingly slow that transformation would be.

"Why did you return? After they got you out. What drove you to fly back into the same danger and spend all those months there again?"

She'd been asked that question dozens of times before, and it was on the tip of her tongue to offer him the same answers she'd devised to deal with it. That immersion journalism gets in your blood. That she was unwilling to leave a job undone.

But because of all he'd offered her, here, tonight, she owed him the truth. "It was the only thing that helped me make sense of it," she said simply. "That's what people do, I guess, when faced with something horribly, unnecessarily tragic. All those people dead, and for what? I wanted something to show for our presence in that hotel. Because if I hadn't after all that suffering, what was the point of it?"

"So you risked your life again so those deaths weren't in vain."

"No." Her voice was sharper than she intended. "You make it sound heroic, and believe me, I was anything but. I was scared all the time. Always. And the only way I got through it was to spend my nights crawling into the bottom of whatever bottle I managed to score on the black market."

"And yet you stayed."

"I stayed." In an alcohol-induced haze most nights, but she'd stayed. She'd remained several more long months reporting on the violence and devastation and then had politely flown back to the States before breaking down completely.

"Few could manage what you did."

The words warmed her, even while she couldn't quite bring herself to believe they were true. Yes, she'd managed to do her job even as she struggled with ghosts that had taken up permanent residence in her mind. And that had been a victory of sorts. But she knew exactly how far she was from vanquishing those specters completely. Charley was right. Coyote *was* always waiting. He was a constant presence inside her, ready to pounce when defenses were lowered.

"I think my ex plans to steal my son."

Shocked at his non sequitur, she twisted her head to look up at him, but Joe's gaze was fixed on the sky. "I learned by accident that she's moved from Window Rock. A private investigator I hired confirmed it. She's living in Phoenix at a furnished condo unit that rents by the week."

"Have you talked to her? Maybe she just—"

"She lied when I called her cell. Mentioned that she'd found a different place in Window Rock that was closer to a park for Jonny." Sarcasm laced his words. "Of course when I asked for the address she skirted that by saying she was planning to bring him here for his visit this coming weekend. She's biding her time. The custody hearing is in a few weeks and the only chance she has to share custody is to remain on reservation lands. But once the hearing is over she'll be gone. It's all she talked about during the final months of our marriage. She wanted us to move away from here, to a larger city, off Navajo lands."

The demand amazed her. "She didn't know you very well, did she?"

He looked down at her then. "And you think you do?"

Though a voice inside her whispered caution, she nodded. "You're a part of this place. It's a part of you. It's not something I can articulate or completely understand. But I know that much." And she envied it, too. What must it be like to have such a powerful sense of belonging? To a place and to a people that shared the same rich past?

"She doesn't know me well at all if she thinks I'll let that happen," he said flatly. "She didn't cover her tracks well enough and I have someone watching her around the clock. For Jonny's sake, I was willing to work out a compromise that would give him some stability with both parents. But she can't have my son."

She could hear the fear mingling with the determination of his vow, and she stroked his chest, soothing the muscles that had gone tense.

After a time he rolled to face her, his hand sweeping down her thigh and then up again, chasing the last remnants of chill from her skin. And when his face lowered, when his mouth settled against hers she gladly twined her arms around his neck, welcoming the embrace.

There was a slightly pagan feeling to making love outdoors, beneath the silent moon and scattered constellations. A sense of wicked pleasure in watching his skin gleam in the thin beams of moonlight slanting across it.

The world narrowed its focus until there was only the two of them, backdropped against the infinite beauty of the night. And when he moved over her, inside her, the breath rushed from her lungs and all she could see was the stars beyond the breadth of his shoulders, his face in the shadows, stamped with the primitive expression of a man claiming his mate.

The alarm shrilling insistently in the back of her mind was muted, but present. Because she knew then, with mingled certainty and sadness, that he was destined to leave a mark on her soul that time and distance would never completely erase.

Chapter 11

"Captain said he wanted to see you as soon as you get in."

Vicki's words greeted Joe and Arnie as they entered the Navajo Tribal Police headquarters the next afternoon. The two men looked at each other. "We just got here," Arnie said.

"Then he wants to see you now."

"I'll be there in a minute," Arnie said, glancing at the clock. "I promised to check in with Brenda. It's the only way to keep her from coming down here and following me around to make sure I don't overexert myself."

"If she thinks there's any danger of you overexerting yourself on the job, she *should* follow you around," Joe suggested. "Be a real eye-opener."

"Yeah, yeah." The other man headed to his desk. "How about some respect for the fallen hero wounded in the line of duty?"

Joe rapped at the captain's door and entered when commanded, closing it behind him on the rest of his partner's good-natured complaints. "Arnie will be here in a minute."

Tapahe gestured for him to sit. "What have you gotten today? Anything?"

The report was depressingly meager. "Nothing on Graywolf or the van belonging to that tread we found. And Lee hasn't returned to his parents' home. Arnie and I have been concentrating on abandoned mines, focusing on a seventy-mile radius, but so far nothing." Time was running out, and this method of investigation was too slow and uncertain. They had approximately thirty hours until the next trip to the border. And he didn't like their chances if they had to sit back and hope Border Patrol spotted the van along the nineteen-hundred-plus miles of border.

"I think we need to get Graywolf in here again." Tapahe still hadn't said anything. "Maybe use that connection to Quintero we established with the cell phone call log and throw in the rumors we've heard linking him to the deaths of those three local youths. He might slip and give us something we can use."

"And maybe he'll be tipped off and the whole operation gets postponed."

Tapahe had a valid point, but the feeling that they were chasing their tails in the intervening hours was beginning to wear on Joe.

Arnie opened the door and joined them. The captain waited until he was seated before continuing. "I think you were right yesterday. We need to get a look at the Graywolf property to decide if we're on the right track before this all goes down tomorrow night."

Joe felt hope stirring. Leaning forward in his chair he asked, "You got us a warrant?"

"Do I look like a magician to you, Youngblood?" the captain said testily. "We've got nothing to take to a judge and you know it. But someone gave me an idea this morning that I think has merit."

Trepidation replaced hope and Joe sat back. "And that someone was?"

"Delaney Carson."

Stunned, he could only stare at his superior. Dimly he heard Arnie ask, "Carson?"

"Apparently some private property owners offered her free access to their land while she was working on the book." He looked at Joe. "That's what took her to the Nahkai property."

He gave a jerky nod, afraid he knew exactly where this was headed. Hoped he was wrong.

"She suggested that maybe Graywolf senior would extend that same courtesy, which would allow her to take a look at that mine you two were interested in."

"No." Fear sliced through Joe with sharp jagged strokes. What if they were right about that mine site? Worse, what if that's where Lee was hiding out? He'd fired at Delaney once and missed. He may not miss the next time.

"I was ready to dismiss the idea myself, but she's a very persuasive lady. And it was a solution to our getting a look at the area."

"That could tip off the kid. Brant."

"I weighed that." The captain eyed him steadily. "Also weighed it against the possibility the elder Graywolf was involved. But you didn't think that was plausible and neither do I. I finally figured her plan might represent our best chance."

"No!" Joe shot up from his chair and braced his hands on the captain's desk. "You're the one who wanted to keep President Taos happy. And now you're thinking of sending her back into a possibly dangerous situation? What if he finds out about it?"

"Sit down, Joe." Their gazes did battle until Joe finally backed away, his jaw tight. He didn't sit. He couldn't. He was too tightly wound for that.

"Carson suggested that she call Taos and ask him to contact Graywolf senior for permission. He got it, probably because Graywolf is hoping for a mention of his company in the book. Whatever the reason, we've got access to the site, and I think the danger to Carson is pretty minimal. Brant would have no reason to believe she planned to be on the Graywolf property today."

"I can't believe Taos would be okay with her walking into a possibly dangerous situation again," Joe said, reining in temper and fear with effort.

Tapahe's gaze shifted away. "I'm sure he wouldn't be."

Comprehension dawned. "You didn't tell him about the investigation."

"*I* didn't talk to him," the captain corrected. "Carson did. I talked to Agents Mitchell and Tarken, and we agreed that what we stood to gain outweighed the slight risk to a civilian."

"Oh, the feds agreed." Driven to pace, Joe strode across the office and back. "I'll bet they did. They've come up with nothing on the homicides and they're desperate for anything that might give them a few answers." He shook his head, aware that Arnie was watching him shrewdly, not caring. "I still don't like it."

"You don't have to like it. It's done." The words had Joe's attention snapping to the captain "Carson and her guide left a couple hours ago."

"You aren't lost again, are you?"

"We aren't lost. We're headed for that butte."

Delaney brought the binoculars up to peer in the direction Eddie had indicated. Distance on the vast lands in the area were deceiving. "Isn't this the direction I told you to go originally?"

"No one likes a know-it-all woman."

She grinned at his disgruntled tone. "Or one that's right. At least I got some great photos of the sheepherders and their flock."

"Always glad to be of service."

She laughed. Captain Tapahe had insisted she not come alone. But she had made sure Eddie was fully apprised of the possible danger. Her caution had been lost on him. He showed even more excitement about the slight risk than he did at the possibility of more billable hours. She hadn't argued when he'd brought his rifle along. After being used for target practice, it didn't hurt to be prepared.

It took a half hour to get close enough for a good view of the looming rocky hillside. They hadn't passed anyone except the two men watching over the grazing flock of sheep. "Take a wide swing around it. Maybe the shaft opening is on the other side."

Eddie obediently did as she asked, though it took another forty minutes to come around the land mass. Delaney brought the binoculars up again, scanning the rough-hewn striated sandstone for anything that resembled an opening. Smaller red rock formations made it impossible to get closer in the vehicle, and obstructed her view. "Slow down." Eddie obediently slowed to a crawl. "I can't really get a good…wait. What are those up ahead?"

Eddie squinted. "Look like old railroad ties. Or what's left of them."

She lowered the binoculars and stared at him. "And what did they use to bring the coal out of the mine?"

"Rail carts." He accelerated until they got to the spot she'd observed then stopped the vehicle. Carefully, Delaney scanned the top of the butte, mindful of the shooter who had remained hidden while he'd taken sight at her on the Nahkai property. But she could see no one. They got out of the Jeep.

The steel rails had been removed long ago, but old rotting ties still dotted a straight path to the cliff face.

Following them with her gaze, Delaney saw the boarded-up entrance of what must be the mine.

Eddie joined her, rifle in hand. "Do me a favor and don't point that anywhere near me, all right?" she said, only half in jest. The place appeared to be deserted, but she knew how deceptive such appearances could be. Although the path along the ties was wide enough to have accommodated the Jeep, the land on either side of it was dotted with irregularly shaped boulders and spears of rosy sandstone reaching skyward, providing ample chances for concealment.

The sheen of perspiration dampening her clothes wasn't owed solely to the temperature. They made their way toward the mine entrance. There was something eerie about their journey, with both of them scanning the surrounding area like jumpy kids in a graveyard.

They reached the closed doors to the mine without incident. Eddie turned to face the vehicle, still wary. "Seems odd," she murmured, pushing against the primitive doors that had been fashioned to block the opening.

"What?"

"There's a new padlock on these doors." The lock was shiny, still gleaming. It hadn't been exposed to the weather for long, unlike the hasp it was fastened to, or the hinges holding the doors to the side beams. "If you were worried about safety, you'd think you'd board the place up completely. Brick in the entrance or something."

Eddie threw a quick glance over his shoulder. "Maybe they still use it for something."

She'd seen no need to give him more information

about Joe's case than she'd needed to. "Maybe they do." Stepping back, she began taking photos of the door, a closer shot of the padlock, and then of the path leading up to it. Something caught her eye, and she motioned Eddie to step aside. The wind was a constant on Navajo lands, but sand collected in places protected by rocks or structures that provided a barrier. It was true here.

There were a couple tire track indentations captured in the light dusting of sand. Because Joe had paid such close attention to them at the cave, she took pictures of each, noting the odd tread apparent on one of them. She eyed the mine entrance speculatively. The tracks seemed to be leading toward, or away from the mine.

She went back to the locked doors, shook them. She could push on either one and get a couple inches gap.

"You want to get in there?"

Just the thought had her palms going clammy. "No." Definitely not. "But those tire tracks had me wondering if there's anything inside."

Peering through the slight opening, she was met by blackness. "Here." She turned, caught Eddie's car keys as he tossed them to her. "Try the mini flashlight on the ring."

Delaney eyed it doubtfully, but turned to press the door open a crack again, shone the tiny beam inside. And immediately caught her breath.

The light glinted off something metallic, something large and solid. Something that looked very much like a bumper.

* * *

"I think it's a match," Arnie observed, comparing the photo Delaney had printed out to one of the tread from the cave site. "Can't be sure without the measurements, of course. What do you think, Joe?"

"It's a match," he said flatly, standing a little aside from the others. Nothing else made sense. The van that had disappeared once leaving the cave site had almost certainly surfaced again, this time on Graywolf property.

This was the break they'd been waiting for, but his excitement over it was muted. He went to the computer screen, brought up the other photos Delaney had taken and clicked through them. The area was remote. Isolated. Fear and anger pierced him when he saw the scattered rocks, any one of which could have provided cover for Lee or someone like him. He looked over at her, talking animatedly to Arnie and Tapahe and felt the anger take precedence. She had no business deliberately taking a risk like that. Not after what she'd already been through.

She glanced his way and her expression froze, her smile slowly fading. A moment later her chin angled and a cool distant mask descended over her features. Their gazes did battle, neither of them giving an inch.

"It's your call, Joe," Tapahe said. "What's your next move?"

With effort, he tamped down the simmering fury and glanced back at the photos in Arnie's hand. There was really only one choice to make. "Let's get the feds back in here. We've got less than twenty-four hours to get this operation planned."

* * *

Joe peered out the window of the DEA Bell 407 helicopter, the high-powered, night-vision binoculars trained on their quarry below. "We've got visual," he announced.

John Honani repeated the information into the radio that maintained contact with the strike forces on the ground.

The van driver had been sighted driving cross-country over Graywolf property just after 6:00 p.m. Once he'd gotten onto a roadway heading south they'd alerted the others to stand by. Customs and Border Patrol had had units ready to mobilize as soon as they could give them an approximate destination.

When the time came, the group of six aliens and the coyote had passed over the remote spot of the border undisturbed, all carrying bundles on their back. Those bundles were probably filled with crystal ice.

The van had waited on the States' side of the border for the aliens to reach it. Once the passengers were loaded, the driver had lost no time heading north again.

"Here." The agent handed him a high-powered rifle equipped with night-vision scope and Joe lowered the binoculars for a moment to study it. He'd never been tempted to join any other branch of law enforcement, but there was no question that the DEA had better toys.

Honani covered the microphone on his headset. "Mitchell wants to get the units in place to take them."

Joe nodded. "Tell the rear flank units to pull within five miles or so, no lights." The combined officers from the Border and Customs agencies would make up those units. "Remind Mitchell to wait until they verify their placement. We don't want to lose the van before we've got them boxed in."

Ten minutes later, the DEA agent shouted, "Showtime!"

The helicopter pilot swooped lower, to hover above the blue van speeding down the deserted road. Honani manned the exterior mike. "DEA. Stop the vehicle immediately." The van swerved slightly, then increased speed. "This is the United States Drug Enforcement Agency. Pull over."

A couple of miles ahead, blinding spotlights were switched on, revealing a barricade across the road, sharpshooters situated behind it.

"You are surrounded," the DEA agent informed those below laconically. "There's another armed unit behind you." The van slowed abruptly to avoid drawing closer to the FBI roadblock. "All passengers should get out slowly, hands in the air."

As the van careened to a halt, Joe looked over at the agent. "Are we putting down?"

"Damn straight we're putting down." A rare grin crossed Honani's face. "I'm not about to miss this party." The pilot veered to the side and began landing several hundred yards to the left of the scene.

When they arrived at the area, officers and agents were swarming all over it. The panicked group of illegals were being separated and patted down. Several agents were searching the interior and exterior of the vehicle. As they approached, Joe was unsurprised to see Tarken and Mitchell questioning the driver, who he recognized as the same guy who had taken off on the ATV at the cave site.

He looked around, expecting to see Niyol Lee. Rounding the vehicle he saw him collapsed against the front driver side bumper, a hand to his heart, with two agents near him. "Sir, do you need medical assistance?" one asked. Lee bent lower to the ground, and the first agent took a step closer.

In the blur of an instant Lee lunged forward, reaching for the agent's gun, even as the second officer swung his weapon higher. But Joe was already at Lee's side, his gun pressed against the man's temple.

Lee stilled, his gaze darting toward him.

"Go ahead," Joe advised him grimly. "Give me a reason."

"You owe me so big. It's going to take a lifetime and you're still going to owe me."

Joe grinned at Arnie's grousing as they made their way to the interview room. "It's not my fault that you didn't have medical clearance. Next time bring a note from your doctor when you want to come back to work."

"Bite me."

"It wasn't that big a deal. You were just as crucial standing by and picking up Graywolf when we radioed in."

His friend's voice was sour. "Yeah, right. You were in a DEA 'copter with special ops equipment, and I got to pull over a guy in a late-model Chevy Avalanche. That's almost the same."

"Did he say anything?"

"Lawyered up as soon as I brought him in. We haven't gotten near him since." They stopped, Arnie's hand on the knob. "Now he's here to play *Let's Make A Deal*."

They entered the room, where Brant Graywolf and a suit were waiting, both seated at a table. Joe nodded at the officer keeping watch over the pair. "Thanks, Danny." The officer nodded and left the room.

"I'm Ruben Filmore from the Tucson office of Filmore, Drake, Conner and Drake." The lawyer was a thin man in his midfifties with a bad comb-over, a pinched mouth and rimless glasses that threatened to slide down his long aquiline nose. "I'd like it noted that Mr. Graywolf is here against my legal advice. And I'll remind you of his right to know what charges are being leveled against him."

"We'll get to that." Joe pulled out a chair, sitting directly across from the younger man. "Tell us why you're feeling talkative, Brant. Against legal advice."

Despite the hours he'd spent in a cell, Brant Graywolf still had a cocky manner. It would never occur to him to face the consequences he had coming. That wasn't his MO.

"I'm willing to tell you what I know of Quintero's operation." Graywolf looked from one to the other, gauging their reactions. "He was a lot bigger than you realize. He was trying to get me to introduce him to my former contacts. I told him I didn't play that game anymore." He shook his head. "That guy had balls, I'll give him that. Or else he was too stupid to realize how many people he was ticking off by expanding so rapidly. Lots of people wanted to take him down for that alone." He gave Joe a nasty grin. "You saved them the trouble."

"Guess we had it figured all wrong then," Arnie told Joe. He looked at the kid. "See, we had you pulling the strings for Quintero. You were the one with the contacts, all right. And you used him to sell the pure ice you were scoring in Mexico."

"Don't know where you guys are getting that. Other than a couple spring breaks in Cancún, I've never even been to Mexico."

"Not you. Niyol Lee."

The lawyer frowned. "Who?"

"No idea who you're talking about, man."

But Joe had seen the kid's eyes flicker at the mention of the name. And he was quickly getting tired of the whole charade. Graywolf hadn't uttered one truthful word since he'd entered the room.

"Maybe your memory will come back if we tell you we've got a book he kept of dates and times you paid him to make runs to Mexico."

Graywolf was swinging his head in denial. "I can't help what he wrote in some book, but if that's all you've got, I don't get why I'm still here." He turned to Filmore. "They don't have enough to hold me. Do something to earn that fat retainer you're getting paid."

The lawyer's mouth screwed up more tightly but he said, "I must agree with my client. Unless you can show some compelling evidence linking him to a crime, you have to release him. I've already submitted a request for bail."

"It'll be denied," Joe said flatly. "You want compelling evidence?" He pushed away from the table, went to the door. "FBI Agent Mitchell has something you might want to take a look at." Mitchell walked in carrying a plastic evidence bag. Joe leaned a shoulder against the wall, prepared to watch the show.

The agent let the bag with the Sig revolver inside land on the table with a thump. Graywolf reared back a little, his face losing color. "Recognize that, Mr. Graywolf?" Mitchell inquired. He looked back at Joe. "Looks to me like he does."

"No." Graywolf recovered quickly. "Should I?"

"Well, I'd think you would. We found it in your bedroom, top shelf of your closet. 'Course there's no law against you having it. Just thought it was sort of a coincidence."

Rather than asking the obvious question, the younger man pressed his lips together and remained silent. Mitchell continued, "Seems the same type of gun was recently used to murder three young men."

"This meeting is over." Filmore stood and tugged at Graywolf's sleeve. The younger man remained immobile. "My client has nothing more to say to you."

Mitchell smoothed his tie, which was stained with whatever he'd had for lunch that day. "I'm guessing ballistics are going to match this gun with the murder weapon. As a matter of fact, I'm willing to bet on it."

He looked around at the other occupants of the room. "Any takers?"

"This is an outrage..." Filmore began.

Graywolf violated a traditional Navajo rule by interrupting. "Shut up." The lawyer looked startled, then slowly sank back into his chair. Leaning forward, Graywolf told Mitchell, "If that gun matches the murder weapon for three kids I didn't even know, someone must have stolen it out of my room. Maybe they're trying to frame me."

"They did a good job," Joe put in laconically. "Yours are the only fingerprints on it."

The kid sat back in his chair, looking from one of them to the other. "I tell you what. You get that list of charges to my lawyer. And the next time we sit down, you have a deal on the table from the federal prosecutor." Filmore looked askance, but Graywolf ignored him. "It's all about the links in the chain, isn't it? You think you followed Oree and Lee to me? If you want a bigger fish, you better come ready to deal. Because my part in this thing is pocket change compared to the rest of this operation."

"You mean the illegal aliens, the slavery ring?"

Joe could tell from Graywolf's expression that his words had hit home. "This meeting is over," the younger man repeated. "I don't have anything to say until you bring me something from the feds to sign."

"What makes you think we need you to find the rest of the links in this chain?" Mitchell said.

Graywolf scraped his chair back and rose. "You

know how I'm sure you'll need my help?" He glanced impatiently at his lawyer, who was slower to rise, seemingly shocked to silence, and then back at the FBI agent. "Because I know how you guys think. You're never going to figure this all out because it'll never occur to you to look at one of your own."

Chapter 12

"Let's call it a night."

Arnie looked up from the report he was typing on the computer. "You look like hell."

Curiously, the blunt pronouncement lightened something inside Joe. "Feel like it, too." He tried to recall the last time he'd had eight hours of sleep. Or even six. He gave up the task as useless after a moment. The last twenty-fours he'd been running on adrenaline alone, but he was about to crash, physically, and he wanted to be in the comfort of his home when he did.

Arnie pressed Save and rose. "You're right. We may as well go home. Everyone else has." Mitchell had left an hour ago. Even Tapahe had finally exited the NTP station forty minutes earlier, and it was rare to be in the building without the other man being in his office.

The two men walked out together, calling a goodbye to the skeletal crew that made up the night-shift. "Do you think Graywolf was blowing smoke earlier? With the crack to Mitchell about never looking at one of your own?"

"I don't know. Graywolf isn't known for his honesty, but even he has to realize that making claims he can't substantiate won't get him anywhere."

"You think he's saying they had some Customs or Border Patrol official in their pocket?" Arnie's words seemed to mirror the direction of Joe's own thoughts. "That would explain them getting away with this business as long as they did."

"He's probably trying to sweeten the deal he's working. I believe him about one thing, though. There's someone above him calling the shots." Joe stopped at his Jeep, his hand on the door. "Someone had to have the contacts in Mexico not only with the cartel, but also to become known as a guide who can get people safely over the border."

"Which could have been Graywolf and Lee."

"Sure." Joe rubbed at his eyes with the heels of his palms. Lack of sleep had them feeling grainy. "But once up here, who had the slavery contacts? Lee? He spent more than half his time living in Mexico. From questioning Martinez, the driver, I have him figured as strictly muscle. And it sure wasn't Graywolf. He's got the drug background but no one is going to trust a young punk like him in an underground slavery ring. He doesn't have the credibility."

"So that leaves…who?"

Joe shrugged. In his mind he'd eliminated the three, but he was no closer to figuring out the identity of their superior. He was too tired right now to try, at any rate.

"Want to stop somewhere and get something to eat?"

"I need to get home while I can still function. Food can wait until tomorrow."

Arnie pulled open the door on his SUV. "You really going home?"

Ready to turn down another dinner invitation Joe replied, "I'm really going home."

"Because I thought maybe you'd be stopping by to see your little *belagana*." Arnie grinned at his narrowed look. "She wasn't any too happy with you when she was here yesterday, but you weren't exactly showering her with gratitude, either."

He didn't want to recall that scene, or the way the hours had passed with interminable slowness until she'd walked into the NTP headquarters. "You don't know what you're talking about."

"I know what I saw. And the sparks coming off the two of you were enough to heat the whole office."

Joe got in his vehicle. "Sounds like you're getting hot flashes. Better go home, Arnie."

"I'm just saying. You might sleep a whole lot better if you first deal with what's really bothering…"

It gave Joe a measure of satisfaction to shut the door on the rest of his friend's words. But the action didn't prevent them from echoing in his thoughts as he pulled out of the NTP lot. He could be thankful for the break in the case that had allowed them to intercept the smugglers while still damning the way it had come about. And if that made him a hyprocrite, he had only to recall his first reaction when Tapahe informed him about Delaney's suggestion.

Anger had been a much preferable emotion to the sick fear that had twisted through him from the moment he heard of the plan until he'd seen her safe again. The relief that had hit him then had weakened his knees and ignited his temper.

Because it wasn't supposed to be like this. No strings meant no emotions, didn't it? He'd been as eager as she for a casual relationship without expectations or promises. The last thing he needed or wanted was involvement with another woman who couldn't hope to understand how interwoven he was in the fabric of his culture.

But he'd gotten her understanding. The memory slammed into him as he pulled into his driveway, of her soft voice full of disbelief. *She didn't know you very well, did she?*

That perceptiveness made him edgy. She saw things other women didn't, from a perspective of suffering few others could imagine.

How could a woman who was supposed to mean nothing to him so quickly become a raging hunger in his blood? How could he, a man of innate caution, have failed to see the risk she presented? Or recognizing it, failed to take heed of the warning?

He stared at his darkened house without really seeing it. The smartest thing to do was stumble to his bed, lose himself in sleep for the next twelve hours.

Which didn't explain why, moments later, he shifted the vehicle into Reverse, and headed toward the town limits.

Delaney stared at the rough outline of the book, mentally adding photos to the future chapters that would accentuate the oral histories and narrative. The actual writing always proved to be the easiest part for her. When it came to choosing the appropriate photos, or worse, limiting how many would make the final cut of the project, she'd agonize for weeks.

But she was a long way from that point. Right now she needed to begin sorting through the photos she'd already shot, putting them in picture libraries according to subject matter so that she could find them easily, deleting the pictures that weren't of the highest quality. She had very exacting standards when it came to her art. In this area, at least, she could control her finished product in a way she wasn't always able to control events in her own life.

Her reaction to Joe Youngblood, for example.

Delaney's blood simmered anew recalling his expression when she's seen him at the NTP station. She'd read the temper in his eyes. His gaze had been as scorching as a laser, and she'd been left with little doubt as to his reaction to her involving herself in his case.

Which was too damn bad. She punched a command into the keyboard with a little more force than was necessary. No man had ever been allowed to dictate her actions and if this was all about tiptoeing around his ego, well, then he had some hard lessons to learn about her.

By the time she heard the knock on her door her temper had gone from simmer to a boil. It was late and she really hadn't expected to hear from Joe, so she took the precaution of checking the judas hole. Recognizing him she pulled open the door and unlatched the screen, spoiling for a fight.

"Can I assume from your visit that you've come to thank me for my help?" she said with mock sweetness. "Oh, wait, I forgot. Joe Younghlood doesn't need anyone's assistance. He's the Navajo's answer to Superman. Tell me." She cocked her head challengingly. "Did you bust that operation you were investigating all by yourself, or did you let your partner help?"

His lips tightened at her sarcasm, but his voice was even when he answered. "There was an entire task force deployed to make the arrests." He walked by her into the room, leaving her to follow.

"A whole task force?" She widened her eyes in mock surprise. "Well, don't feel too bad. Even superheroes occasionally let their sidekicks in on the action."

The muscle in his jaw was clenched tightly. "They were all law enforcement. Professionals trained to handle dangerous situations."

"Is that what this is about? That I'm not a cop?" She gave a short laugh. "Be honest. It's because I'm a woman." She ignored the dangerous glint in his eyes, to continue. "I've got a news flash for you—I've been making my own decisions for a few years, now. I even manage to dress myself daily without help."

"You deliberately put yourself into a high-risk situation," he said, anger lacing his words.

"Well, your captain disagreed with you about the risk."

"You got lucky. No one was at the site, but you didn't know that. And neither did he. You could have been shot at. Maybe hit this time, killed. Did you weigh in those factors at all when you dreamed up this idea?"

Her voice raised. "Or I can get hit by a bus crossing the street. If people sit home and assess risks all day, they never accomplish anything."

"I don't care about 'people'," he bit out, shoving his face to hers. "I care about you! More than I should. Do you know what I went through, waiting to hear from you?"

"I didn't ask for that," she whispered. Her throat dried out abruptly, her temper squelched like quenched flame. She took a step away from him, and then another. "I don't want that."

She couldn't be responsible for his feelings. She wouldn't be. It was bad enough recognizing that she'd gotten involved with him deeper, faster, than she'd ever thought possible. Whatever emotions he dragged to the surface inside her, however, she'd handle them. But she couldn't handle *his*. Couldn't manage the guilt and recriminations that would invariably follow her failure to be what he wanted. *Who* he wanted. The thought of having to try scared her to death.

"You think I want this?" His face was a mask of

frustration. "That I was looking for it? My personal life is a shambles and the last thing I need right now is to fall in love with a woman I just met."

"This isn't love," she interrupted, a little wildly. Denying it loudly enough, often enough, could make the words true.

"The hell it isn't." He strode over and caught her arm. "It's love when I'm sick with fear until you show up safe and sound at the station. And when I think about you even though my mind should be occupied with the case. Maybe neither of us planned on it, but we're in deeper than we ever intended to go." She tried to turn away, but his hand on her arm stopped her. "Yes, we are. You can't deny it and neither can I. Now the question is, what are we going to do about it?"

It must be due to some genetic flaw in her makeup that she preferred his temper to his emotion-roughened voice. His tone had turned low, his touch caressing. As if he understood that his angry declaration had her wanting to flee from his feelings. From her own.

"You can't run away from it, Delaney. I know you better than that. You don't run away from much in this life, do you?"

He was crediting her with a bravery she didn't deserve. The flashbacks of the bombing of the Iraqi hotel weren't the only memories that had left scars. There were the still-fresh recollections of what it meant to love a man who could only give her leftovers of himself. And what was left of Reid after he'd poured most of his energy and emotion into his work had never satisfied. She wasn't sure what had scared her more—the thought that someday she would have walked away from him, or that she would have settled. And lost a little of herself in the process.

"Look at you." Was that amusement in his voice? Her gaze flew to meet his. "You'll walk into the middle of a war-torn country for a story, but right now you look terrified. Is it that bad, admitting you…feel something for me?"

She didn't miss that hesitation in his words. And she certainly didn't mirror his amusement over this scene. "I don't know how to do this," she said rawly. "I don't know what you want from me."

A measure of tension seeped out of him. His thumb skated over the sensitive skin above her palm. "I don't want anything you don't give freely. Nothing has changed."

But she knew that wasn't true. Everything had changed with this conversation, not the least being that she was nearly paralyzed with panic. "I need to think."

"No. You need to *quit* thinking. So do I." He drew her closer, his arms looped around her loosely, seeming not to notice the stiffness in her limbs. Or determined to ignore it. "I handled this badly. We don't have to have this conversation now. We'll just see where things lead. It doesn't have to be more complicated than that."

But he was wrong and they both knew it. Sex was uncomplicated, relationships weren't. Invariably emotions ruined everything, changed everything. It was only a matter of time before they had to deal with that.

The thought pierced her with a sliver of the pain that surely was to come.

But not tonight. She could read the exhaustion on his face. There was no way to solve this now, and really, what was the point? She already knew how it would end. Best to back away from the declaration he'd made and pretend, at least for a time, that it didn't alter everything.

She strove for a steady voice. "Does this mean I don't get to see you in your tights and cape?"

"Keep it up, Carson." He nuzzled her neck. "I may be tempted to show you some of my superpowers."

"I'd be interested in seeing those myself." They both jerked, as the screen door opened and a figure stepped inside, pointing a gun in their direction. "Barring that, I'll settle for a little information."

"What the...Bruce?" Joe released Delaney and turned toward his ex-father-in-law, automatically placing his body between her and the gun. His mind responded sluggishly as he struggled to reconcile the unfamiliar sight of the mild-mannered schoolteacher with an automatic pistol, complete with silencer.

"You kept me waiting, Joe." Bruce Glenn moved into the room, his gaze going from him to Delaney and back again. "We could have handled this just between the two of us if you'd shown up at home. As it was, I had no choice but to follow you out here."

"Whatever this is about, we can still handle it between the two of us." Carefully, Joe took a step toward the other man, halted when the pistol was raised and pointed toward his chest.

"It's too late for that. I don't have much time and you have something I need. So both of you will have to come with me."

Eyeing the man speculatively, Joe wondered if he'd gone over the edge. His entire demeanor at the NTP station had been off, but he'd figured Bruce had just been upset about his lack of contact with Jonny. He'd showered the boy with attention since his birth. But now…he was acting entirely too comfortable with that gun, and Joe had never known him to have one before.

"Just tell me what you need." The number one rule in volatile situations like this was to keep the gunman calm. But he also wanted to get the man away from Delaney. "I can't help you if I don't know what you want."

Bruce's smile was chilly, and completely unlike him. "What I want is my grandson. You're going to take me to him."

Joe's fingers clutched the steering wheel in a grip that made them ache. Bruce had insisted they take the SUV he'd arrived in, one Joe had never seen before. Checking the rearview mirror again, he met the other man's gaze. "She's fine," Bruce said, indicating Delaney, who was seated next to him, bound and gagged. "She'll remain that way as long as you cooperate."

He wished desperately that he could shift the mirror's position to see Delaney's expression. Professional instincts warred with all-too-personal emotion, and he couldn't afford to be distracted by it. But emotion had reared the instant the man had stepped into Delaney's house and pointed a gun at her.

"Why don't you tell me where we're going?" he asked with a calm he was far from feeling. "Seems simpler that way."

"Just follow my directions. You've already made things more difficult than they should be." The man's voice sounded with frustrated fury. "I know you've discovered where Heather took Jonny. Did you call your cop friends when you figured out Heather was no longer in Window Rock? Or did you go looking yourself?"

Thinking furiously, he said, "Heather's not in Window Rock? Are you sure?"

The pistol was slammed against his head, hard enough to have him veering on the deserted road. "Don't play games with me. I've already waited hours and I'm out of patience. Where did you find her?"

Distant headlights shone ahead, the first they'd seen since they'd left Delaney's. Joe slipped one hand lower on the wheel, closer to the lever controlling his brights. Maybe he could flick his lights at the driver. At the least they might call in to report a possible impaired...

"Don't even think of trying to alert that driver. It'd be a shame if I had to hurt the woman just because you did something stupid."

"This is crazy, Bruce. I miss Jonny, too, but there are easier ways to get to see him."

"You're a little slow on the uptake today. I'm not just going to see him. I'm taking him with me."

Time crawled to a standstill. A horrible suspicion

bloomed, too illogical to be given credence. "Where are you going, Bruce?"

"I think I'll keep that detail to myself. But I don't have much time, do I, Joe? How much longer do you think it will be before Graywolf spills everything he knows? He'd sell his grandmother for the right price, and I'm guessing he thinks the price of his freedom is my life."

The truth hit him with the force of a careening bus. Bruce? Involved with Graywolf? Disbelief filtered through him. "What do you know about Brant Graywolf?"

The man's expression in the rearview mirror was one he'd never seen before. Calm, matter-of-fact, cold-blooded. "I took precautions. A man in my line of work has to. But an operation is only as strong as the links in its chain and once things start to disconnect it doesn't take long to bring the whole thing down around your head. When I didn't get the call from Graywolf telling me Lee's run was successful I knew I didn't have much time. I went to your house to find the address for my grandson, but you didn't write it down, did you, Joe? You're a careful son of a bitch, I'll give you that. Turn left here."

"This isn't a road."

"Turn left!"

He gave a sharp turn of the wheel and they bounced over worn ground. The time for pretense was over. "There's no way I'll let you take my son."

"You know, I knew that'd be a problem," the man said conversationally. He was leaning forward to watch the uneven terrain carefully. "But turns out you provided your own incentive." He reached over and grabbed Delaney by the neck, pulled her close enough so Joe could see the gun pointed at her forehead.

"Now this would be a tough choice for anyone. But I overheard enough of your conversation tonight to be pretty sure you'd like to keep her alive. And the only way to do that is to give me what I want."

A paralyzing fear encased Joe. He couldn't be asked to choose between his son and Delaney. No one should have to make a choice like that. Somehow he had to figure out a way to save them both.

"Turn right. It's only a few miles."

The Jeep jolted over the uneven ground, and Joe wondered again where they were going.

"Why don't you call Heather now, Bruce? Talk to your daughter. To Jonny. You've got to see that this isn't the way to solve things."

"Heather's made her opinions clear," he retorted. "Why do you think she left the reservation? She doesn't want Jonny contaminated by me. But he's *my* grandson! She's made her choices. Now I'll make mine."

Joe's heart seemed to stop, then slowly picked up speed again. Heather had known about Bruce's activities. Or at least had suspected enough to send her running with their son. All this time he'd believed she left to be ready to run if she lost custody. Instead, she'd been protecting Jonny, in her own way.

It wouldn't have been Joe's way. Anger ignited like a match to a fuse. She could have come to him. Gone to the police with what she knew. Instead she'd chosen to shield her father from the consequences of his actions.

And now her choice just might return to haunt them both.

"There, up ahead."

Joe peered out the window, but with no regular road to guide him, he was unclear just where he was. He didn't normally travel reservation land as the crow flies. All he could see up ahead was the dark silhouette of a rocky butte. But he heard the sound Delaney made and was suddenly certain he could guess the site.

The abandoned Graywolf mine.

"Police have been swarming all over this property. We need to go somewhere safer, Bruce. Somewhere we can talk."

"The police are long gone. Why would they keep it under surveillance when our cargo was intercepted? It's the perfect destination. Because we both know they have no reason to come back."

Joe's mouth dried and desperation ricocheted through him. Unfortunately the man was right. The members of the task force had no idea who they were looking for at this point, and no reason to believe that Graywolf's boss would head back to the very place they had planned to stash the illegals.

Joe and Delaney were on their own.

His palms were slippery on the wheel as he slowed at Bruce's command. He had a sudden premonition of just how this was going to go down and the scenario wasn't pleasant. His best chance was to try and overpower the man, but Delaney's presence made that trickier. She gave Bruce leverage. And she represented a weakness for Joe.

"Turn left here and stop. Leave the lights on and the vehicle running."

He made the mistake of turning to look at Delaney. Her gaze was fixed on the mine, and her eyes looked as though she were peering into the gates of hell. He could see the shudders already racking her body and knew she understood what the man intended.

Bruce reached across her and opened the door, then, with his hand gripping her arm, roughly shoved her out of the Jeep. "Get over here, Joe."

Adrenaline balling in his stomach, he rounded the front of the Jeep and caught Delaney as Bruce gave her a push toward him. "You two stay in front of me. She'll remain in the mine and you'll come with me. Call her my insurance policy."

Joe didn't have to feign difficulty propelling Delaney toward the mine entrance. She had her heels dug in the ground like a person on their way to the gallows. And if he let himself think about the terrifying panic she was experiencing right now, neither one of them would get through this alive.

Joe gave her shoulder a reassuring squeeze. There was no way he'd leave her to fight her demons alone inside that cavernous shaft, but they *were* going to have to enter it. Grimly, he hoped he could transfer a bit of reassurance through his touch but doubted it would penetrate her sheer terror.

When they reached the mine entrance, a quick burst of hope unfurled. It was unsecured, a sawed-through lock lying at the foot of the doors.

Bruce saw it and muttered an oath. "Open the doors."

Joe pushed one door forward, and then the other. The hinges screeched with age and disuse and he had to catch Delaney in the next moment, as her knees seemed to go to water. "It's going to be all right," he whispered urgently as he held her upright. But she didn't seem to hear him. Abruptly, muscles that had seemed lax only a moment ago seemed filled with extraordinary strength and she fought frantically, with single-minded determination to break free of his grip and flee this confrontation with her darkest fears.

"Control her, Youngblood or I'll shoot her where she stands."

It was only the certainty of that threat that would make Joe catch her and swing her around, moving her inexorably into the mine's entrance. "It'll be all right," he whispered the litany in her ear as he held her tightly before him. "I promise it'll be all right."

Delaney could hear his voice but the words meant nothing to her. The only thing she was aware of was the yawning blackness that was drawing closer with every step. Her blood had turned glacial, her throat closed with horror. Her frenzied struggles were instinctive, involuntary. She couldn't go in there. She knew if she did, she'd never come out alive.

It was like being struck blind, every ounce of light blocked by fallen debris and twisted metal. The interior shrinking until each molecule of oxygen seemed sucked away to leave her to gasp and fight for every breath. She'd die like the rest of them, screams turning inhuman as the certainty of her death loomed closer.

"Find something to use on that latch for the doors. I want your girlfriend staying put while you drive me to get Jonny."

"I'll give you the address." Something in Joe's voice filtered through the fog of Delaney's fear. "You go and we'll both stay here."

"Nice try. The only way to be sure you'll give me the right address is to have you drive me there. And keeping the woman here gives you a little incentive to follow directions. Stop right there."

There were three quick thuds in succession. With superhuman effort Delaney strove to focus on the present, as the past threatened to drown her in a sea of terrifying memories. Blinking, she saw that bullets had been fired into one of the timber supports near one side of the mine, splintering it.

"All right, Youngblood. Back away from her and go pick up one of those fragments. One of them should work in the clasp."

Delaney stared at the timber, but what she saw were twisted metal beams awash in plaster dust and portions of stone supports, bodies pinned beneath.

Desperately, she beat back the memories, focused on the man's voice. If she concentrated on something other than *the yawning pit of darkness waiting to swallow her up* she could think of a way out of this.

She watched, transfixed, as Joe moved as if in slow motion. Her mind ping-ponged between a kernel of hope and utter despair. There was no way out. He bent, reached for the piece of wood. It was a miracle she'd lived the last time, and how many miracles did one person get in a lifetime?

She was aware he'd risen but her gaze had moved past him, just a yard or two to where the interior of the mine turned to inky shadows, as deep and impenetrable as a grave.

Her grave.

The hypnotizing darkness seemed to exhale, brushing her skin with its chilly breath. When it inhaled it'd suck her in, feeding on her panic like a vulture gorging on a carcass. And live or die, she'd be broken. Spirit, mind, body. *So much easier to accept it.* The specters of the past sounded like frigid whispers in her mind. Just walk into its frosty embrace and let it happen. *I'm so tired of fighting. So tired.*

Mesmerized, she took a step forward, eyes wide. There were images stamped on the darkness now, mental fragments that had lingered in her nightmares for two long years. Another step forward, and the past hurtled toward her with the power of an oncoming locomotive.

"Move it, Youngblood."

The snap in the voice filtered through her trance and

she stopped, looked around confusedly. And saw Joe staring fixedly at her, saw his lips moving.

She forced herself to look away. He couldn't distract her now. Not from this. It was too important. Desperation and acceptance warred inside her. Muscles tensed. Time slowed.

And then she whirled, diving for the man with the gun. "Sonofabitch!"

She'd lost track of him in the darkness. Instead of hitting him square, her body struck him in the thighs and he stumbled back, his legs tangled with hers as they both went sprawling to the ground. Delaney threw her weight onto his gun hand, felt pain explode as his free fist caught her in the face once, twice.

Then she was free of him with a suddenness that, along with the ringing in her ears, dizzied her. She rolled away, struggled to her knees. And saw Joe and Bruce entwined, rolling, exchanging blows. One clipped Joe in the chin and his head snapped back. But even as Bruce reached for the gun that had slipped his grasp, Joe drew back a clenched fist and plunged the sharp wood fragment he still held into the man's eye.

The scream that bounced through the mine's interior was an eerie echo from the past. The memories threatened to rush in, reaching for her with eager clutching fingers. But Delaney was moving, racing to retrieve the weapon.

She had an inkling of what Joe saw when he looked up then, a wild-eyed woman holding the automatic weapon in surprisingly steady hands. She recognized the concern in his expression. His grip on

Bruce loosened, as he slowly, cautiously rose, keeping his gaze on her face as he held out his hand for the weapon.

There was a single terrifying moment when her mind replaced him with an apparition that lingered from the nightmare of her past. But an instant later her vision cleared and he was there again. Grim, competent and amazingly unhurt. Gingerly she handed the gun to him. An instant later his free arm reached out to haul her close, and a tidal wave of relief slammed into her, turning her bones to water.

"You did good, 'Laney," he whispered as they watched the man writhing in pain on the ground. "You did real good."

The blanket around her shoulders should have warmed her, but Delaney's form continued to be racked with shudders. Her mind, though, was clear as she watched the police work the scene.

The place was swarming with law enforcement, and once she'd rejected the need for medical assistance, the ambulance had taken Bruce Glenn away and left her alone. In the bustle of the crime scene she was all but forgotten as she leaned against the fender of a police unit. Except for one man, who paused frequently to send a concerned glance her way.

The police units' headlights had the area lit up like near dawn but she kept her gaze carefully away from the mine hulking in the background. She didn't want to consider how easy it would have been to succumb to its chilly embrace.

The aftermath of the ordeal continued wreaking its private misery. The warmth of the blanket couldn't quite chase the chill from her skin. Her heart refused to regain a normal beat and her stomach was a twisted mass of clenching nausea.

But she was still standing. She wasn't sure she could do it without support, but she was on her feet. She'd faced her darkest fears, and she'd done it without the help of a bottle of Absolut. She'd celebrate her private victories in the tiny increments with which she achieved them.

She didn't fool herself that there wouldn't be further repercussions from this experience, but she did believe she'd weather them without reaching for that bottle on top of her cupboard. It wasn't a drink she wanted right now, at any rate.

Joe detached himself from the group of officers and headed toward her. She noted his searching gaze, and thought he realized just how close she'd stepped to the abyss. For once the thought of allowing someone near enough to know her that well failed to terrify her.

"I've commandeered one of these rides. Are you ready to go home with me?"

She stared at him, her mind filled with a sort of clarity that had been missing for longer than she could remember. "Yes." She pushed away from the car and walked toward him. "I think I'm ready."

Epilogue

"You missed! I win again!"

Jonny's jubilant whoop cut through Joe's reverie as he bounced the basketball to his son. "You're the champ, all right. Want to go for three out of five?"

The evening air was still warm enough to have them both perspiring. They'd shed their shirts an hour earlier. Maybe with the workout Jonny would be exhausted enough to go to bed without a struggle. It was a good thought, even if he didn't hold out much hope of it.

His son had gone through a lot of adjustments in the last year and a half. It had only been recently that Joe felt as though he could stop scrutinizing the boy for any signs of trauma over the changes in his family unit. Kids were resilient, far more so than adults, although Joe had undergone a few major changes of his own.

He checked his watch. Thirty minutes to bedtime. He rebounded for his son and pulled up for a short jump shot. When he missed, he turned his son's jeer into a groan by announcing, "Time for bed. You just have time for a shower and a snack if you hurry."

"Come on, Dad! Another fifteen minutes?"

Looking down in his son's eyes he steeled himself against the familiar con and said, "You know the rules. Doesn't matter if you're at your mom's house or mine. Summer bedtime is eight-thirty." Although the theatrics didn't diminish, something in his voice must have convinced the boy because he started trudging toward the house.

Joe retrieved their discarded shirts and went to put the ball away. It had been difficult to forgive Heather for what she'd planned to do. Even after hearing her tearful explanation of wanting to get Jonny far away from the monster her father had become, it had been tempting to let it all spill out at the custody hearing. By revealing that she'd learned of her father's activities and systematically planned a way to run, rather than go to the police, there would have been no contest to the hearing. She may even have faced jail time. She might have deserved that.

But his son didn't.

The scandal that had swept the reservation when Bruce Glenn's activities had come to light would be hard enough for Jonny to grow up with. He didn't need to lose his mother in the process, as well.

Joe headed toward the house. It had taken nearly a year, but he and his ex had come to a wary sort of truce. She'd taken up residence in Chinle and Joe was as fair as he could be with the time she spent with Jonny. It had been over six months since Graywolf had been sentenced, and four since Bruce's trial.

And it had been three months eleven days since Delaney had left.

The familiar longing traced through him as his mental calendar notched another day. She'd stayed put longer than he should have expected. Perhaps the most remarkable of the changes he'd undergone had been a gradual understanding that he could no more ask her to stop doing what she loved than she would have suggested he stop being a cop.

So he'd stepped aside when she'd taken that new job, swallowing his protests, his worry, and learned to live with the gut-clenching desolation that had been a constant companion since she'd walked away. He had his son. His family. His job. It should have been enough. But ever since she'd left there had been an acid-etched void that no one else seemed capable of filling.

Joe walked over to pick up Jonny's bike, wheeling it closer to the house when an unfamiliar car slowed and pulled into the driveway. Frowning, he turned and lowered his son's bicycle.

"I didn't know superheroes rode bikes." Delaney slammed the car door and rounded the hood. "Another myth bites the dust. One of these days I'm going to completely lose every ounce of naiveté I hold dear."

He was at her side in two quick steps, his arms closing around her. "You didn't tell me you were coming back this week." He kissed her, long and deep, before raising his head to get his fill of looking at her. "We would have come to the airport to get you."

"I wanted to surprise you." He looked good, she decided, staring hungrily at him.

"You've got the book done already?"

He hadn't released her and that was fine with her. Leaning against him, she murmured, "I've got enough material, I think. And if not, I can always fly back for a quick follow-up."

The sordid tales that had emerged from the Graywolf and Glenn trials had ignited her imagination. Following her completed project on the Navajo culture, she'd decided to go to Mexico for an in-depth study of the staging society that existed near some border crossings. Although Joe hadn't been able to hide his reaction to her plans, he hadn't tried to dissuade her. At least not much. But even in his silence it had been an excruciating decision to leave, even for a time. And the loneliness she'd experienced in the intervening time away had shortened the time she'd spent on the project.

"Dad!" A bellow from the house interrupted them, and they looked toward the six-year-old boy, clad only in his underwear, framed in the doorway. "Can I have some ice cream? Hey, 'Laney's back! Did you bring me something?"

Laughing, she called back, "It's in my bag." He whooped and ran back into the house. "It's a carving of Huitzilopochtli, a deified ancestral warrior-hero."

"Did you bring me anything?" The suggestive timbre in Joe's voice had a delicious shiver chasing over her skin.

"Just me."

His face lightened in a rare smile. "That happens to be exactly what I wanted." There was a look in Joe's eye, seductive promises that she was anxious to test. "I can't wait to have you all to myself." But then he glanced toward the house and said, "But first I have a six-year-old preparing for the nightly bedtime battle."

"I know. I can wait."

"Really?" His tone was light, but there was a flicker across his expression. "I was kind of hoping we were done waiting."

She looked at him without answering. She knew he was asking about their future, and it was a question they'd learned to avoid since her answer only seemed to bring them both pain. But that was before she'd spent three long months away from him. The gnawing pain of missing him had clarified a great many things she'd once had trouble understanding for herself.

"You're right." She stopped and waited for him to face her. And wanted desperately to erase the cautious mask that had slid over his features. "You have waited. I'm sorry for that. I thought…" She struggled to find the words.

There had been a time in the not-too-distant past when she'd thought she'd never have a sense of belonging to any place. Or anybody. That to do so would mean losing a part of herself. But as soon as she'd set eyes on Joe again, the certainty that had been growing in her over the last few months had bloomed. She belonged here. With this man, wherever he was.

"It doesn't matter what I thought. I love you, Joe Youngblood." The savage joy on his face ignited an answering emotion and when his arms closed fiercely around her, she hugged him just as tightly. "You had to wait too long for me to say it. To realize it. But I don't think you'll have to wait long to hear it again."

"Good." He cupped her face in his hand, his eyes searching hers. "Then we're done waiting?"

"Yes." They headed toward the house, arms wrapped around each other's waists, gazes locked. "We're done waiting."

* * * * *

RUN, ALLY! Don't be fooled by him. He's evil. Don't let him touch you!

But as the forbidding figure came through the mists toward her, Ally knew she couldn't run. His features burned with dark malevolence, and his physical domination of everything around him seemed to hold her like a net.

She'd heard the tales. She knew all about the Wolverton legend and the ghost that haunted The Willows, an elegant old mansion lost by Micha Wolverton nearly a hundred years ago. According to folklore, the estate was stolen from the Wolvertons, and Micha was killed, trying to reclaim it. His dying vow was to be reunited with the spirit of his beloved wife, who'd taken her life for reasons no one would speak of, except in whispers. But Ally had never put much stock in the fantasy. She didn't believe in ghosts.

Until now—

She still didn't understand what was happening. The figure had materialized out of the mist that lay thick on the damp cemetery soil. A cool breeze and silvery moonlight had played against the ancient stone of the crypts surrounding her, until they joined the mist, causing his body to thicken and solidify right before her eyes. That was when she realized she'd seen this man before. Or thought she had, at least.

His face was familiar. . . so familiar, yet she couldn't put it together. Not with him looming so near. She stepped back as he approached.

"Don't be afraid," he said. His voice wasn't what she expected. It didn't sound as if it were coming from beyond the grave. It was deep and sensual. Commanding.

"Who are you?" she managed.

"You should know. You summoned me."

"No, I didn't." She had no idea what he was talking about. Two minutes ago, she'd been crouching behind a moss-covered crypt, spying on the mansion that had once been The Willows, but was now Club Casablanca. And then this—

If he was Micha, he might be angry that she was trespassing on his property. "I'll go," she said. "I won't come back. I promise."

"You're not going anywhere."

Words snagged in her throat. "Wh-why not? What do you want?"

"If I wanted something, Ally, I'd take it. This is about need."

His words resonated as he moved within inches of her. She tried to back away, but her feet were useless. "And you need something from me?"

"Good guess." His tone burned with irony. "I need lips, soft and surrendered, a body limp with desire."

"My lips, my bod—?"

"Only yours."

"Why? Why me?" This couldn't be Micha. He didn't want any woman but Rose. He'd died trying to get back to her.

"Because you want that, too," he said.

Wanted what? A ghost of her own? She'd always found the legend impossibly romantic, but how could he have known that? How could he know anything about her? Besides, she'd sworn off inappropriate men, and what could be more inappropriate than a ghost? She shook her head again, still not willing to admit the truth. But her heart wouldn't play along. It clattered inside her chest. The mere thought of his kiss, his touch, terrified her. This wildness, it was fear, wasn't it?

When his fingertips touched her cheek, she flinched, expecting his flesh to be cold, lifeless. It was anything but that. His skin was smooth and hot, gentle, yet demanding. And while his dark brown eyes were filled with mystery and wonder, there was a sensitivity about them that threatened to disarm her if she looked too deeply.

"These lips are mine," he said, as if stating a universal fact that she was helpless to avoid. In truth, it was just that. She couldn't stop him.

And she didn't want to.

* * * * *

Find out how the story unfolds in…
DECADENT
by
New York Times *bestselling author*
Suzanne Forster.
On sale November 2006.

Harlequin Blaze—Your ultimate destination
for red-hot reads.
With six titles every month, you'll never guess
what you'll discover under the covers…

Silhouette®

nocturne™

HER BLOOD WAS POISON TO HIM...

MICHELE HAUF

FROM THE DARK

Michael is a man with a secret. He's a vampire
struggling to fight the darkness of his nature.
It looks like a losing battle—until he meets
Jane, the only woman who can understand his
conflicted nature. And the only woman who can
destroy him—through love.

On sale November 2006.

nocturne™

USA TODAY bestselling author

MAUREEN CHILD

ETERNALLY

He was a guardian. An immortal fighter of evil,
out to destroy a demon, and she was his next
target. He knew joining with her would make
him strong enough to defeat any demon.
But the cost might be losing the woman
who was his true salvation.

On sale November, wherever books are sold.

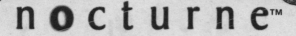

nocturne™

Save $1.⁰⁰ off

your purchase of any
Silhouette® Nocturne™ novel.

Receive $1.00 off

any Silhouette® Nocturne™ novel.

Available wherever books are sold, including most bookstores, supermarkets, drugstores and discount stores.

Coupon expires December 1, 2006. Redeemable at participating retail outlets in the U.S. only. Limit one coupon per customer.

5 65373 00076 2   (8100) 0 11265

SNCOUPUS

Silhouette®

nocturne™

Save $1.⁰⁰ off

your purchase of any Silhouette® Nocturne™ novel.

Receive $1.00 off

any Silhouette® Nocturne™ novel.

Available wherever books are sold, including most bookstores, supermarkets, drugstores and discount stores.

Coupon expires December 1, 2006. Redeemable at participating retail outlets in Canada only. Limit one coupon per customer.

52607136

SNCOUPCDN

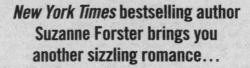

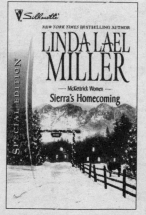

INTIMATE MOMENTS

#1439 CLOSER ENCOUNTERS—Merline Lovelace
Code Name: Danger

Drew McDowell—Code name Riever—is curious to know why a recently fired defense attorney has developed a sudden interest in a mysterious WWII ship. When the mission takes a bizarre twist, the two must work together, while fighting an attraction that threatens to consume them both.

#1440 FULLY ENGAGED—Catherine Mann
Wingmen Warriors

Pararescueman Rick DeMassi never thought the woman he'd shared an incredible night with years ago would be his next mission. But when a stalker kidnaps her and his daughter, this air force warrior must face his greatest fears and save the two most important women in his life.

#1441 THE LOST PRINCE—Cindy Dees

Overthrown in a coup d'état, the future king of Baraq runs to the only woman who can help him. Now Red Cross aide Katy McMann must risk her life and her heart to help save a crumbling nation.

#1442 A SULTAN'S RANSOM—Loreth Anne White
Shadow Soldiers

To stop a biological plague from being released, mercenary Rafiq Zayed is forced to abduct Dr. Paige Sterling and persuade her to team up with him in a race against a deadly enemy…and their growing desires.